The Guard and the Princess

Lucy Tinsley

Contents

Chapter 1

"Princess!" As a nobleman approached, footsteps resounded down the great hallway. The Princess who was in front of me tensed but made a polite turn in its direction. She briefly blinked her eyes at me, and I restrained a smirk when I noticed how annoyed she was.

She addressed the audience with "Sir Oro," a slight head-up. Her back was covered with chic curls from her pitch-black hair. With my hand resting on the hilt of my sword, I took a position two paces to her right and behind her. A familiar location. "What else can I do for you?" Although her smile appeared genuine, I could tell it was constrained and uneasy.

Before the aristocracy in front of him, the man bowed. As he rose, his eyes swept her from the ground up, and the Princess gave me another annoyed expression. A few minutes earlier, I heard her stomach rumbling painfully, and I knew she was returning to her room to eat in private. The annual ball will begin later this evening, and I was wondering if the Princess would be interested in dancing.

She gave a polite nod. "I'll think about it." She quickly made a U-turn and headed for the west wing of the castle. The man's eyebrows dropped as he looked at me after speaking to her for only one line. I gave a quick bow to the nobleman in front of me before turning and following the Princess by two paces. Sir Oro's own footsteps, which were now moving in the opposite way, were being drowned out by the swishing noises that her dark green garment was making.

I was able to keep up with the Princess and kept a watch on all the people passing by, including couriers, guards, and servants. All the way to her apartments, people were making the customary quick bows. She curtly nodded at the speakers after hearing a few 'my Princess's'. The Princess was standing next to me when I opened the door of her room, which was made of dark oak. The sound reverberated around her room as I closed it behind us.

Princess Seattel's bed had pillows that Helen was already fluffing when she entered the room. I assumed my usual position in front of the double doors, placing one hand on my sword's hilt and the other down to the side. Helen gave me a quick look before turning to the Princess, and I smiled a little.

"My grace, do you need anything else?"

Princess Seattel sighed and massaged her temples. Do not refer to me as that.

"My apologies," the Princess's maidservant responded. Before the princess could see, she gathered a vase of flowers from the side of the bed and crumpled the paper. My sneer intensified. It was obviously a gift intended to wow this prince from a gentleman. Helen put the paper in a tiny trash can off to the side as she followed Princess Seattel. She growled at me, but she could not stop a smile from spreading across her face. The question "Is there anything else?"

"Thank you Helen. Simply put, I want some peace. She collapsed on the bed in a most unprincesslike manner. Do you realise how many men have lusted for me today? She started removing the pins from her hair and giving them to Helen when she was ready. "My ears are ringing,"

"Your grace, that is what happens when you are old enough to get married." I smiled and gestured in the direction of the worn-out royal. The Princess rolled back onto the bed and groaned once more. Helen moved a pillow from under her head in an effort to be of assistance.

Do not refer to me as that.

I said, "Your grace, my apologies." Helen rolled her eyes, stared at me once again, and brushed Princess Seattel's hair while fully aware that I could continue to address her by her formal titles.

The twenty-year-old told the Princess in front of her to ignore that man. He is making an effort to annoy. The maidservant observed the princess as she ran her hands through her hair while standing back. Do you want to take a bath?" That might lessen your headache.

I grimaced. Princess Seattel was experiencing head pain, but I had forgotten. I informed Helen, "She does need some nourishment. "While she was meeting all the gentlemen, her stomach grumbled."

The palace has been bustling for a few weeks. Servants and maids hurried between rooms as they prepared for the yearly ball. But it needed to be distinct from previous years this year. Princess Seattel was now eligible to get married because she had turned 20. Of course, everyone received an invitation, but only a small number responded with no misgivings. Men from all around the world visited the Princess. Each person considers the possibility of courting the Evergreen Princess.

In the opulent hallway, the princess had been positioned next to King Yakima, her father. I had positioned myself behind her as usual, watching out for any danger. The monarch and his daughter would greet each invitee, and this year there were a lot of them.

There were knights and royals. There were a few elderly guys and even some noblemen vying for her affection. This time, I restrained my grin as I recalled an elderly nobleman approaching the princess as she was preparing to welcome him to the realm. She extended a hand in greeting to the man with white hair. He appeared to be having sex with her hand. She then gave me a stealthy glance as he moved away, and despite my best efforts to conceal it, she must have noticed the laughing in my eyes.

Helen started to dart about the space. She questioned Princess Seattel, "Wine, juice, or water with your meal?"

"Water."

Helen bowed to the girl who was lying there. To let the maid escape, I slightly opened the door made of dark oak. Helen began to murmur to me before I could close it. Was it really as horrible as she had feared?

Even though I felt horrible, I smiled and shook my head. "I think it was even worse," It had been more than two hours since the initial welcomes. This time, I banged the door shut softly before turning back to face the princess. My other hand, which had been on the hilt of my sword, now at my side.

The royal girl moaned, "Food," clutching her stomach. I grinned wryly.

"My grace, would you like me to wait outside the door?" I queried. The room quickly warmed up as the sun emerged from behind a cloud, casting light across her bed and into her eyes. She opened her eyes and rolled them away from the light to look at me.

She emphasised my title, "Sir Washeen," "No, sir." "I'd rather have you stay in this room with me so I can irritate you with my never-ending whining." She took a few steps to arrange her clothing and sighed once more.

Is that a command or a recommendation? For the past four years, I have served as her personal guard, so I understood how to react. She did not appreciate it when those she regarded as friends used her titles, but I have always done so. Obviously, she had to do it in public even though she detested doing it. It was difficult to break the habit.

"A command."

I stayed where I was in front of the doors. Standing up, Princess Seattel went to her table. She questioned me, asking "How many men do you think came this year that did not come last, just to see if they can woo me?" A few of the flowers in the arrangement on the table were touched by her fingers.

I laughed. There are "quite a few."

She gave a scowl. They were all so wrinkled and aged. The orange that was sitting in the fruit basket in front of Princess Seattel as she sat down at her table was peeled open. The fruit made my mouth start to wet. They were a rare pleasure for regular people. I had only ever sampled a half-piece.

Princess Seattel, a royal, was accustomed to eating such wonderful fruits. They were such an expensive treat because they were imported from lesser kingdoms. She fired the question at me, jolting me out of my reverie, "Did you particularly like any of them?"

I shook my head as I thought of some of the odd men. "I believe Sir Leavenworth or Sir Oro was the best, in my opinion.

Until Sir Oro admired you in the corridor, that is, your grace. She trembled as I watched.

She met my hazel eyes and admitted, "I thought he was okay too. "Definitely younger, and not that ugly. But now that he chased us down the corridor, I think he may be in a dire situation. She savoured the orange while she nodded her agreement. "Why do you think that, Sir Leavenworth?"

I told her, "He is a very high nobleman." "From what I heard, he was a great strategist, young, and respectful." I raised an eyebrow at the Princess. And he didn't wet your hand, either. At the thought of that other elderly man bathing her hand with his tongue, she wrinkled her nose. "He didn't look weird; he just seemed kind and interested. I've heard that he is fair to his employees as well.

Prior to relaxing more on the chair, Princess Seattel flicked her black hair over her shoulder. "You raise some really good points. Everything feels so overpowering. She averted her gaze. I don't want to attend the ball tonight. I had the impression that I could sleep for weeks.

As I turned to let Helen enter, three fast knocks echoed around the space. I clenched the handle of my sword even though Helen always knocks on the door in the same manner. Since there were so many foreigners in the town and castle, I must admit that I felt a little more uneasy.

Helen was there, though, holding a hot bowl of soup. I allowed the housekeeper in. "My grace, may I suggest that Sir

Washeen keep watch outside the door?" The princess heard Helen's words. We have to get you ready for the ball tonight." She handed the princess her spoon and carefully laid the scalding hot bowl down.

Princess Seattel waved her hand at me and gave me a gentle smile. I crept out the door and found a seat outside the chamber, where I observed the maids and attendants scurrying about in the hallway. My hand was resting on the sword's hilt.

A familiar location.

Chapter 2

As gracefully as her layered gown would allow, the Princess made her way into the ballroom. Behind her, the magnificent red dress shimmered as it moved across the floor. Her contour was followed by a chic halter neckline all the way to the slightly puffed out skirt. The neckline was outlined in diamonds. Her back was perfectly outlined by a corset, and a ribbon tied it all together.

The group of single males and a few more fell silent quietly. The King took a position to the left of his lovely daughter and cast a commanding glance in all directions. Naturally, I was two feet to Princess Seattel's left and behind her.

Announcing professional cleaned throat. "King Yakima and Princess Seattel of the Evergreen Kingdom, his majestic daughter." The dialogue resumed as the King took his daughter to their places at the head table as the musicians to the left of the audience rolled into a sweeping musical composition.

As a man drew near Princess Seattel, she flashed me a frantic glance. As Sir Oro bowed before the Princess and the King, I gently narrowed my eyes at him. I would be honoured, Princess Seattel, if I may take the lead in the first dance.

King Yakima spoke to the excited nobleman before she could reply. "Should we partake of the feast before requesting a dance?" The players' flutes seemed to get louder as they played.

Sir Oro made another bow. "Yes, my King, we will. I only wanted to know if the Princess was aware of my earlier this morning's query. Regarding the aristocrat in front of him, King Yakima scowled. He moved forward with a meagre but commanding step.

Are you saying that my daughter is incapable of remembering anything?

I observed Sir Oro start to quiver slightly. "N-No. Not at all, my King. The gentleman then moved away deftly. "Your majesties, enjoy the feast." He bowed once more before hurriedly turning around to face his own table.

Princess Seattel once more accompanied her father to their dinner. As she passed, she muttered, "Desperate," in my direction. I refrained from grinning as I turned and followed her gracefully to her seat. The King didn't indicate that he had observed his beloved daughter acting in such an unacceptable manner. I moved to the side to make room for her grace to sit in the chair. Once everyone was seated, the King motioned with his arm for servants to enter via the side doors with plates of vegetables, various kinds of meats, and boiling pots of stew.

Before the guests, tables with pig roasts, chicken legs, even beef meatballs, were set up.

I was a few steps behind Princess Seattel, my hand resting on the hilt of my sword. As a few too many drinks were consumed, chitchat and laughing started to echo through the hallways. With flowers and fireflies in jars as decorations, the candles and lanterns flickered across the room. The King made a small inclination towards his daughter.

"Seattel, I'm sorry, but Beaverland's prince told us this morning that he couldn't attend the ball this year. His finest is sent. The King bit into a chicken leg and began to chew.

Seattel scowls. However, Eugene adores these yearly feasts. On her plate, she began to pick at some raspberries. I'm aware that this caused the princess a great deal of sorrow. Prince Eugene and she share a similar age and have interacted frequently. They are, as one would say, two sides of the same coin, yet neither of them is in love with the other. They came to a mutual understanding, and I was present to see them make the commitment.

Each individual requires a good friendship.

The King stroked his daughter's beautiful hair from behind her as he put his hand on her shoulder. Only a simple diamond head chain was there tonight, following the part in her long, flowing hair. On her brow, a flawless diamond is perched. His envoy reported that the Prince had made other plans before we were invited. Princess Seattel gave her father a nod.

Sir Leavenworth roared with laughter as he leaned over the table, filling the entire room. A section of the pig roast was covered by a strand of his longer blonde hair. His tunic's sleeve had a stain on it. The aristocrat took another swallow of the vivid red liquid that was in his cup. Princess Seattel fixed a strand of her hair and purposefully shifted her body a little to the left. Her clear eyes met mine.

They talked with me. He is inebriated.

My lip corners twitched upward slightly in an attempt to apologise. She sighed loudly but quietly while her eyes narrowed. Her hair began to fall back down behind her as she turned around. One of my gloves was mended. Princess Seattel nodded in appreciation as Helen moved closer and filled my princess' water glass from the side.

The first dances went just as expected—painfully well. Sir Oro repeatedly attempted to intervene, Sir Leavenworth was more inebriated than a skunk, and the elderly nobleman couldn't keep his eyes to himself. As I watched from the sidelines, I grimaced internally as man after man approached the Princess and offered her a fun dance. Princess Seattel grinned and extended a fair and cordial invitation to dance to each man. a real monarch. After several foot stomps and twists, she politely denied the next dance, stating that she would rather a drink.

Before any male could offer to buy her anything, Helen poured her some of the red wine.

How far along are the improvements, my Princess? As I pushed her chair in for her, I questioned the Princess, who was red-faced. She gave me a stern look as she took a classy drink from her glass. In front of her, she set the glass on the serviette.

Good work, Sir Washeen.

I took a step back to my starting position and nodded as I rested my hand on the comfortable hilt of my sword. The Princess huffed and then turned a little to face Helen. "I guess I should dance a little bit more." Sir Oro stared at Princess Seattel before setting down his mug and approaching her from the left as the music seemed to have picked up a little. I made my weapon more secure in my hands.

Again bowing low, he said, "Your grace."

He received a constrictive smile. The title "Sir Oro."

Can I have this dance, please? I'd give him that much cred-it for persevering—the man did not. Helen gave me a quick glance, her only indication of humour being a slight twinkle in her eye. I'm sure Princess Seattle had complained to her about him moving closer to her in the corridor. I gradually turned my gaze back to the environment in front of me.

Princess Seattel rose up without saying a word and extended her hand to the nobleman after Helen helped her get dressed. She softly placed her hand on his arm while wearing a white glove after he appeared to quickly pick up on the signal.

The princess's gaze briefly flew to mine as the song shifted to a gentle rhythm and Sir Oro danced to his right. Did she like this song? this motion? Who is he?

No.

As her bodyguard, I wanted to pull her out of that unpleasant situation, but sadly, doing so would not be perceived as 'saving' and 'protecting' her.

And that is what I do. Even though I am certain that she would value it.

As King Yakima spoke to a nobleman at his right, my attention was diverted. Both males were drinking while they stood off to the side of the dance floor and observed the dancers. The ladies were swept off their feet as vibrant dresses danced about the grounds. Compared to previous years, "my daughter seems quite interested in the men this year." The nobleman agreed with the king by nodding.

I nearly choked on the water I was drinking, but I managed to maintain a perfect stance despite my short, fast breaths. If only the King were aware of his daughter's true thoughts.

Sir Leavenworth stumbled into the dance between the princess and Sir Oro and asked to join in and dance with her elegance as I watched. Sir Oro reluctantly abandoned his dance.

I widened my eyes in disgust at Sir Leavenworth's unworthy behaviour as he put his hand on the princess' lower hip. When Princess Seattel slightly raised his hand, the music grew once again and a catchy, bouncy tune started playing.

I was startled out of my thoughts once more. The nobleman gushed over the younger girl, saying, "She looks absolutely stunning, your highness." "Truly beautiful." The monarch grinned.

"I hope her attractiveness attracts a strong man. To help her finally lead this empire, she will need a person who is both tactically and physically capable. The King took another sip after stroking his beard and swirling the drink in his glass.

Please pardon me if I go too far, my lord, but Prince Eugene would make the perfect match for her suitor.

The King seemed unaware of his daughter's distaste for the intoxicated Sir Leavenworth as he watched as she was spun by him a touch too roughly. The King of Beaverland and I were both appreciative when they told us they would continue to be friends. I observed as a servant brought the King another glass while he took another sip. "My daughter will rule both Prince Eugene's Beaverland and my realm. Attempting to combine the two kingdoms would be messy. They could forge a peace agreement that is even more powerful than the one I and the Beaverland King could since, in my opinion, their bond is unbreakable.

The nobility gave the King a nod of approval. I will therefore concur with your wishes and hopes that Princess Seattel will find a capable man.

My gaze scanned the space before returning to the princess. Once more switching partners, she was now dancing with a powerful knight. My gaze briefly turned back to the King, whose features became more cheery. I was sidetracked by Princess Seattel's sincere chuckle.

She appeared to be enjoying this dance.

The King asked the nobleman next to him, "Who is that?" I caught Helen's eye as well, and I raised my shoulders a little to show that I didn't know the man.

The gentleman introduced himself as "Sir Coulee" to the king. One of the best knights in the east, born of pure aristocratic stock. We giggled as we watched Princess Seattel spin about with the knight with the dark brown hair. He was reportedly one of the knights who resisted the Gem's approaches, from what I've heard.

This truth kind of impressed me. Our eastern neighbours were the Gems. They were brutish, vicious savages who took everything they pleased. They invaded our Kingdom a month ago, which caused fear because our men had just been ordered to the south a few weeks earlier. Only a small army, led by a few knights who had volunteered, was left to protect the communities. These knights heroically led the army against what appeared to be an insurmountable foe while fighting gallantly.

Their victory at the Battle of the Ruby Tiger was and continues to be the hot topic of conversation. I observed Princess Seattel smile at the partner she was dancing with while tossing her hair back over her shoulder. I pulled again on my glove.

Another round of chuckles ensued as he grinned back at her and continued.

Chapter 3

My thoughts exploded from my dreams as the alarm went off. My muscle memory allowed me to quickly get dressed without even realising I was awake. I pushed the doors to my chamber open as I grabbed my sword from the wall pegs. I broke into a dead run and continued straight down the dismal hallway towards the dark oak doors of my Princess. I could hear yells of anguish in the hallway below and heard clanging.

I hoped my feet wouldn't stumble.

I threw open the doors. I turned and raised my sword in defence towards the door while disregarding how they struck the brick wall. Helen was gazing in from the entrance to the maid quarters, which was attached to the side of the Princess' bedroom, out of the corner of my eye. "Get her dressed!" I said. As the sounds coming from the hallway became more audible, I yelled her way. The Princess walked over to me as Helen fled off into the wardrobe.

Mr. Washeen! What is going on? The moon was the only source of light in the nearly completely dark chamber.

"Return now!" I shoved her away in Helen's direction before turning around and assuming another defensive position. To make sure I still had the dagger in my boot, I quickly looked down. My eyes glanced briefly to the left, where Helen tossed a black dress over the princess, who was still wearing her night-gown, as clothing was thrown out of the closet.

I could hear the clashing of the blade. They were approaching.

"I'm still wearing my pyjamas," As Helen fastened a leather belt around her, squeezing it tight against the princess's trim waist, Princess Seattel exclaimed.

"There is not time!" I hissed at the females. Princess Seattel's hallway was suddenly filled with the voices, and a few arrows were streaking across the vacant area. The sound of metal rubbing against metal caused the mirror in the vanity stand to tremble, eliciting cries and another intake of pain. Princess Seattel put on some of her outside boots, and Helen let out a tiny peep.

I looked into the corridor. A man in black stabbed one of the guards in the chest with a blade that was glittering with blood. His face was marked with a smirk. He ran past the second guard as his bloodthirsty eyes shifted to his next victim. The young guard heard an agonising sound and saw his life flash before his eyes as he looked down.

Say "Sir Washeen!" Helen dialled my number in a panic. Turning around, I noticed the Princess wearing a black dress and cape with her hair tied back under a hood. She clutched a tiny dagger that was accented with a few rubies because she was terrified and her hands were trembling. I looked at Helen.

Without saying a word, I grabbed the Princess' wrist and started to drag her out of her chambers behind me as I fled. I never made sure Helen was following. My biggest concern is for the Princess.

As we ran down the hallway that had seen a battle, shouts were exchanged. It was evident to run in that direction because the one road was free of men. Someone shouted "Get her!" behind us, their voice harsh and raspy. Something was tossed down the corridor, and there were a few hollers and shouts along with a huge crash. The wall-reflected torchlight matched the rhythm of my heart's rapid heartbeat.

I swung the Princess in front of me and looked behind me to see two men running towards us. I gave her another shove. "Run!"

Although her boots and outfit flowed behind her, her trousers were loud. She accelerated a bit.

Her head was whistled by an arrow. It was too close to handle safely.

I didn't waste any time and leaped, grabbing her by the waist and dragging her into another hallway. This time, she didn't require assistance as she pulled herself together after the quick turn and started sprinting along the empty walkway. The path was still lined with light and firefly jar remains. I moved in front of the fleeing heiress to unlock the heavy doors that were blocking the way.

Another combat was going on inside the former ballroom by the opposing doors. Before setting some seats in front of the doors, I moved the Princess back once more. I hoped the men in black would have to work hard to get through. The stench in the room was similar to the one that would haunt my dreams—a mixture of perspiration and blood.

My mind was racing with ideas and a tactical survival plan for the Princess.

Which men were these? Resistance? Gems? Embarrassed Badland Bandits?

After we leave the palace, where should we take the Princess to ensure her safety? The woods? the closest town? even outside of the kingdom?

Some of the folks I recognised were from my training class. Some of the combatants were knights, some were merely trained noblemen, and some were palace guards. Sir Oro was delivering punch after blow to the adversary while clenching his teeth and grasping his ribcage. Blood was all over Sir Leavenworth's face as the knight quickly spun and stabbed a brute in the shoulder. As clangs reverberated throughout the ballroom, I made sure the Princess was safely hidden behind me.

My gaze quickly shifted to the ballroom's third set of doors. a final exit. A second arrow hissed by and sank into the doorframe. Princess Seattel exhaled heavily and grabbed my arm. She trembled.

My attention was drawn to a scream of pain as Sir Oro was stabbed directly in the abdomen. Before Sir Oro replied by skewing the enemy fighter through his own gut with his boot blade, the hostile warrior let out a horrifying chuckle.

They both passed out. As Sir Leavenworth attempted to retreat from the conflict by dragging a hurt Sir Oro behind him, an arrow entered his leg, and I took a trembling breath. The opposing blade pierced the man's heart, and he died before he could even scream. His demise.

"Sir Washeen!" exclaimed my Princess. Her clear eyes enlarged at the sight, and she appeared to be crying a little bit.

I didn't waste any more time hesitating. I yanked the Princess towards the final exit by grabbing her wrist once more. She held onto my arm. Behind us, another scream reverberated. The doors squeaked in protest as I pushed them open. Two troops were drawn to it from the ballroom. My teeth were clenched.

Four more people came down the hallway. Sir Chelan and Sir Everett charged at the guys in black while Sir Chelan yelled a battle cry. They appeared to have exited a room off to the side of the hall. The lower arms of each had scratches, and Sir Chelan was wearing just one boot. The two knights managed to avoid an arrow that one of the enemy soldiers fired from an arm-mounted equipment. I firmly set the Princess behind me and removed her trembling fingers from my arm.

The life of Princess Seattel was in jeopardy. My familiar sword's hilt was grasped, and I assumed a defensive position. I served as the Evergreen Princess' personal guard.

Fighting was the only option available.

Chapter 4

As adrenaline flooded my body, I took in the scene from a tactical perspective. Helen, too, had appeared from the chamber behind Sir Chelan and Sir Everett. She grasped the Princess and pulled her close, away from the horrible scene that was about to take place.

I was facing two warriors, both about five paces away from me as they charged through the open doors of the ballroom we had just left. Their eyes were bloodshot, and saliva droplets were spewing from their mouths, which were open with ghastly roaring. One of them wielded a crudely made and rusted sword, while the other carried a gore-encrusted mace in both hands. I knew that on the other side of my grace, Sir Chelan and Sir Everett were facing twice their number as well, and one of those four had a strange wrist-mounted arrow device.

In confidence, one of the men in black roared, "Long live the Gems!"

Lunging forward, sword in my right hand, my left hand took hold of a loose wall chalice on the hall, ripping it from the mortar. Without hesitation, I flung it at the Gem warrior who had the mace in both hands. The hot wax of the chalice splattered across his face as the chunks of mortar and metal of the chalice holder mashed into his nose and left cheek. He roared in fury and staggered back as the burning wax smashed into his new facial wounds and his hair caught fire.

In that moment, the other gem warrior swung his sword in a wide arc, and its serrated edge tore through my lower left arm. I felt a horrid ripping sensation as muscle and skin were shredded by his attack, and my arm began to immediately pulse with sharp pain as blood began to stream from the gaping wound. But adrenaline kept me going. With a retaliatory surge of wrath, I gripped my sword even harder in my right hand, and bashed the pummel into his jaw, feeling the sickening crunch of shattering bone and teeth as the steel of my royal blade smashed through his barbaric mouth parts. The warrior staggered back, clutching his shattered jaw as broken bits of jawbone and teeth sprayed across the brick wall behind him. Without hesitation, I plunged my sword into his gut, wrenching it to the right, disemboweling the Gem brute as he collapsed onto the floor.

At that moment, I heard a fearsome roar, and felt a rush of air leave my lungs as a heavy body slammed into my own, sending me sprawling on the ground. His face coated in hardened wax and bits of mortar, parts of his hair burnt, the mace-wielding barbarian lunged on top of me, using the handle of his mace to press my neck into the floor. A swift kick of his heavy boot sent my sword scraping across the floor away from my right hand, which grasped wildly for anything to use as leverage against the brute. My vision clouded as the handle of the two-handed mace was pushed harder against my windpipe, restricting airflow. His face was right in my face, and I felt the heat of his angry breath as he roared an unintelligible curse in my face, spraying saliva, blood, and chips of wax over my face.

In a last ditch effort to get his crushing weight off of me, I shoved my right knee upward into his side, knocking him off balance. The weight on my throat subsided long enough for me to catch a breath, before he lunged downward again. But my knee moving up was all I needed. Grasping wildly with my right hand, I felt the hilt of the small dagger I had in my boot. As the barbarian roared in fury, I shifted it out of its sheath and into my hand, using a swift motion to jab the dagger repeatedly into the Gem warrior's ribcage. His roars became gasps as the squealing of burst lungs escaped from the wounds I had made with the dagger, which was coated in blood and torn veins. As he wavered, I used all my force of both arms, despite the pain on my left, to shove him off me and onto the floor. As he lay on his back, he laughed through his pain. My boot slammed into his neck several times, crushing his own windpipe in retaliation and snapping his neck.

I couldn't see my sword. My vision was blurred with blood and wax, but there was no time to look around. Princess Seattel and Helen huddled together in the hallway in horror, having just witnessed my performance in the brutal spectacle that is often referred to as "honorable combat" by many knights.

Charging past them, I saw Sir Everett grappling with a Gem warrior. They both had blood-coated daggers, and seemed to be stabbing each other in the limbs as they tumbled across the hall. Sir Chelan was swinging a massive claymore sword at two of the other Gem warriors in a fury only to be described as battle-lust, as they ducked and dodged his wild swings, attempting to lash out at him with their short swords. But one Gem had been overlooked. He stood farther back, fumbling about with his wrist-mounted device, seeming to load another small arrow-like shaft into it. I couldn't let him get another shot off.

With a leap, I kicked my feet forward and slammed them into the chest of this last Gem warrior. We both fell to the floor, but he was nimble and quick. With a roll, he was on his feet, and so was I. He swung his left fist low and fast, into my stomach, sending a ripple of nauseating pain through my torso. In retaliation, my right elbow swung in an upward arc into his jaw, and I heard the crunch of teeth clashing together as he staggered back. With all the strength I could muster in my torn open left arm, I grabbed his upper right arm, while my right hand took hold of his right wrist, which was fitted with the strange shooting device. With a lunge and a twist, I forced his right hand up to his chin, pulling the little latch on the device as I did so.

The arrow fired with deadly intent, impaling him through his mouth and into his skull. He staggered back again, collapsing onto the floor as blood and bits of broken skull pulsed from his open head wounds. His body made several spasms, and then laid still.

At this moment, Sir Chelan had finished a mighty swing, severing the legs of the two Gem warriors he had been facing. They both collapsed to the floor, screaming. Sir Chelan didn't bother to finish them off as they writhed in agony. Instead, he whirled about to face Sir Everett and his foe, who had been rolling about on the floor this entire time, lacerating each other repeatedly with their daggers. Using his claymore as a great lever, he pried them both apart, sending Sir Everett rolling backwards to lay on his back on the floor, panting. He then slammed the hilt of his great claymore into the face of the exhausted Gem warrior, who, from the force of the blow, slammed against the lower wall of the hall, gasping in shock. A second bashing of the claymore handle crushed the facial bone and half the skull of the man, anointing the hall and Sir Chelan's hands in blood and shattered bone fragments.

My Princess and Helen were crying in fright, turned inwards to each other as if in an attempt to unsee what they had seen. Sir Chelan laughed, and extended a gore-encrusted hand to Sir Everett, who shakily took it, and struggled to stand. I looked about quickly, locating my sword which had slid to the side in the chaos. Lunging forward, I scooped it up in my right arm, ignoring the searing pain in my left arm and the bruises my body would no doubt have by morning. I felt the grime and wax smear off my face as I ran my hand over my eyes, so that I could see more clearly. Helen's nightgown had a few spots of blood stuck to it.

"Princess, are you alright?" I first checked the health of Princess Seattel. She nodded, tears gathering in her eyes. Her gaze went down to my forearm. Pain throbbed through my muscle and bone as the injury caught up with my racing mind. I gritted my teeth.

"We must keep moving!" I grunted.

"But Sir Washeen! You are hurt. We must get to the physicians!" Princess Seattel shakily spoke, the bottom of her chin trembling. She turned to Helen and hastily whispered, "He is losing a lot of blood." The torches in the hallways casted shadows all around us, making her glance around skittishly.

Helen ripped off a piece of her nightgown before tying it around my wound and pulling it tight. It burned and I begged myself not to make a noise. Sir Chelan and Sir Everett had kicked the bodies to the side of the hallway and were barely standing, blood dripping from wounds in so many places, I could not keep track.

"There is no time, my grace!" I spoke through clenched teeth, fire pain raging throughout my body. I forced myself to stand straight and focus on the terrified Princess in front of me. "We must leave the castle." There were echoes of swords clanging somewhere nearby and the princess flinched every time the metal hit. Sir Chelan grimaced, but picked up his sword and stood behind the Princess, eyes darting down the hallway.

I began jogging, holding the wrist of the Princess in an iron grip. She had no choice but to keep up with my pace. Helen was close behind her, with Sir Chelan and Sir Everett taking up the rear. Dodging certain areas littered with bodies and other areas with screams of pain, I managed to lead the group to the tunnel exiting the castle to the south. I made sure the Princess was safe, once again, before kicking open the secret door to the outside. The wind blew fiercely and I brushed my reddish-brown hair out of my eyes before clambering up the small hillside.

"Move quick!" I hissed toward the rest of the group. The hillside had no trees and no cover as we hustled up the steep side. The grass whipped against my trousers as I clutched my arm. The moon was bright and the sky was clear. Sir Everett and Sir Chelan kept silent as they glanced over the castle walls, watching for the men in black. Those filthy Gems. Smoke billowed from inside the walls and my heart felt a stab of dread.

The city was burning.

There was a sharp whistle and a yell as I turned around, leaping onto the Princess and covering her with my own body. Another arrow hissed through the air. A gut-wrenching gasp was heard and seemed to echo around the entire kingdom.

Princess Seattel muffled a scream into my shoulder as I forced her to stay down.

Helen fell into the grassy field, dead, an arrow protruding from her heart.

Chapter 5

"**H**ELEN!" The shriek came from Princess Seattel. I lost my grip on the Princess as she squirmed her way out from under me. She hit my arm and I fought back the black spots that swam into my vision. "NO!" She ran to the redheaded girl and yanked the arrow out, pressing her palm into the bloody wound.

Sir Everett threw himself in front of the distraught heiress. An arrow pierced his leg. The Princess did not seem to notice as she hugged the body of her best friend. Her black hair dipped into the red liquid. Her sobs were heartwrenching.

"Idiots!" came a voice from the city wall. "Our orders are to capture the girl, not kill her!" A few whoops echoed the hillside as I slithered through the longer grass, eyes on Princess Seattel. The roars of the Gems were loud. They were coming.

The Princess wept over the girl. "Helen!" I grasped the Princess and threw her behind me, sheltering her from enemy sight. A Gem roared. "Helen!" Her voice cracked and her crystal eyes leaked tears. Her body shook in my grasp and she uttered more hoarse words. "Wake up!" The gruff voices of the Gems carried on the wind. A few clambered up the hill and into our line of sight, practically drooling at the sight of the Princess and her worth in coin.

"Charge them!"

"Get the Princess out of here!" Sir Chelan bellowed as he pulled the arrow out of Sir Everett's leg. The latter knight screamed as fiery pain flowed up his leg. Gems continued to flood out of the castle and Sir Chelan raised his sword, running to intercept their path. He was outnumbered for sure, but I admired his bravery. Sir Everett, unable to move, still clutched his sword to his side and prepared for his first swing.

I turned sharply around and grabbed the Princess under her legs, throwing her over my shoulder and making a run up the hill towards the woods. Four arrows shrieked past my legs and buried themselves into the hill. Her hip bone pressed uncomfortably into my shoulder. She shrieked, punching my back. "We can not leave Helen!"

"Princess! Be quiet!" I was harsh with my words. There was a moment of silence from her as horrible sounds echoed the hillside. Her body trembled.

A throaty grunt from Sir Everett signaled the end of his life. There was one more sword clang before the sound of metal hitting flesh finished off the last of the Evergreen knights. I forced myself to ignore the hot liquid running down my arm as my bandage bled through and grasped the body of the Princess tighter than before.

"Do not shoot! You might hit the princess!" My feet pounded up the hillside as I finally made it into the forest. The woods were ironically peaceful, with some wind and the moonlight shining through the treetops. However, the stomping feet of twenty or more soldiers kept me moving, nimbly and carefully dodging roots and branches. The Princess continued to sob.

After running for a few minutes, my breaths were coming quick and hard and my lungs felt like they were going to burst. I had no choice but to put the Princess down and make her run with me. I knew that this was not the ideal situation, but yet if I continued how I was, I would have no energy left to fight if need be.

I gently dropped her under a small ridge with moss and roots covering most of the entrance. She hiccupped. "Shush!" I put my hand over her mouth. I listened closely as a few footsteps ran by. "My grace, you need to be quiet!"

"Sir Washeen!" she cried softly. "We left Helen!" I understood she was in shock, but now was not the time to be grieving for our friend. Her breath was caught in her throat as she stared in horror at the blood on her hands. She began frantically wiping them on the moss that laid in front of her, having a small panic attack. I had to calm her down quickly. "I demand we go back!"

"Listen," I held her arm tightly. Her frantic eyes met mine and I wiped a bit of blood off her cheek. "Helen is dead. She died an honorable death and although we cannot go back and get her, she will be dearly remembered." I shook her arm a little. "We need to keep running. If we can make it south to Beaverland we can take refuge there." A little sob interrupted me and we both froze, hearing another pair of footsteps coming close. They paused, then continued down the forest. Once again, we were plunged into quietness with a few screeching crows. "My Princess, you need to focus. We need to start running south." It was almost a minute before I was sure that she had heard my words.

"I demand we go back!" She turned her head away from me and stuck her nose slightly in the air. Her black hair was long and wavy down her back, tangled from the ordeal it had just gone through.

I sadly shook my head at the distraught girl. "You cannot demand that. I am in charge of your safety and if I need to haul you over my shoulder once again, I shall do that."

She glared at me hard. She huffed but before she could turn away once again, her eyes widened. "Sir Washeen! Your arm!" I looked down to see the blood dripping through the bandages. I grimaced.

"There is no time for that right now. We must get you to safety." Her eyes filled with more tears but this time she held them in. This time, she accepted what I said.

I listened closely and peeked out from our spot. We could hear a few Gems shout in the forest farther away and I knew this was the best time to move before they could pin our location. I stood and offered her my hand. She gave me a watery smile and allowed the help up. "Keep your footsteps silent," I instructed her.

She nodded. I pulled a twig out of her hair before turning, placing my hand on her wrist and helping her walk with me. We moved silently, but quickly, through the woods.

There was a crack behind us.

I unsheathed my sword and in a heartbeat, yanked Princess Seattle behind me, placing my forearm on the man's neck, blade making a small cut. I used my weight to pin him against a tree. "Die, filthy Gem!"

"Woah! It is I! Sir Coulee!" came a slightly familiar voice. I did not budge my sword an inch, turning slightly and using the moonlight as a torch. The man had dark brown hair and a cut above his eyebrow, blood smeared across part of his face. A green cape was wrapped around his shoulders and a silver colored chainmail tunic hugged his body.

I cocked my head slightly. "Sir Coulee?"

The knight let out a shaky breath. "Yes, it is I. Can you please release me?" A shout came from behind and I whirled around to see a Gem soldier running full speed at us. His sword was raised and I released Sir Coulee and held my sword a little lower, swiping up at the soldier. The tip of my blade left a long scratch up the brute's cheek. Sir Coulee pulled the Princess behind himself and held his sword at the ready. This particular

Gem must not have been as well trained as the ones we fought in the hallway as I was able to defeat him in a few simple moves.

Princess Seattel stood shaking behind Sir Coulee. She looked at me, frightened, and I narrowed my eyes at him. "She can stand behind me," I spoke sternly. I took a hold of her arm and gently, but quickly, moved her in my direction.

Did I trust the man in front of me? Yes. He was a knight of the Evergreen Kingdom. However, the Princess was my responsibility and I preferred to be the one protecting her with my life as I knew I would not fail to sacrifice myself.

The knight raised his hands in innocence. "Excuse me. I was trying to be helpful." I gave Sir Coulee a curt nod of gratitude and Princess Seattel placed her hand in the small of my back. The familiar warmth fired up my senses once again and I listened for trouble. There was another ghastly howl from a Gem soldier close by and my gaze darted to Sir Coulee.

"We need to move."

"This way!" A Gem soldier screamed our location to his comrades.

Once again, the Princess and I began running through the woods and thickened bushes. Sir Coulee took up our tail and although my heart was racing with adrenaline, it was slightly more calm knowing someone was watching our back. Princess Seattle's dress was snagged a few times in the thorns and as I ripped it away, making sure to not leave pieces of fabric behind, I thanked the stars that Helen had dressed her in black. My heart ached for a moment before I shoved the feeling deep down.

I would never see her again.

I pressed on.

We ran for a few hours. Whenever we thought it was safe to take a minute and catch our breaths, there would be another soldier shout and once again, we would run. A few times Sir Coulee stayed behind to fight a couple of men but he masterfully conquered each foe and continued on with us. I could see how the knight won the Battle of the Ruby Tiger.

I held back a grunt of pain as my wounded arm was snagged on a branch. Sir Coulee glanced at the wound and back at me, grimly nodding. He and I both knew it was a bad slice and it needed a physician's attention in the next little bit. We paused one more time, Sir Coulee giving the Princess his water canteen and then placing his hands on his knees and gasped a bit for breath. Princess Seattel nodded her thanks toward the knight before gulping some of the cool, refreshing water. My own throat ached, longing to feel the moisture enter my own body.

"Do you believe we have lost them?" Princess Seattel questioned, eyes darting nervously around the woods. Once again, it seemed peaceful but we all knew better than to trust the chirping birds. The sky was beginning to light. I looked at the purple and dark red color, knowing we would be a lot easier to spot in the morning brightness.

"For now," I supplied the Princess with relief. "However, I believe we should keep walking for a few more hours."

Sir Coulee nodded his agreement toward me. "Sir Washeen is right. If we have lost them now, our best bet is to get in a few more hours of walking. Chances are they will double back and retrieve horses to chase us down more easily." The Princess handed him his water canteen back and I winced at the look of her black hair. The tangles would not come out easily.

I froze as a cracking sound echoed around the trees. Slowly, I unsheathed my sword and turned around. There, in a small clearing, was a deer. It was nursing a small baby. I released a shaky breath and as I went to put my sword back into the sheath, I noticed I could not bend my arm that way. I looked down and winced as the wound was indeed looking bad. Sir Coulee raised his eyebrow at me, but did not say anything to me as I swapped the sword into my other hand and sheathed it.

However, Princess Seattel had noticed and she glared at me. "Sir Washeen! What did I say?"

"Princess," I bowed slightly to her. "It is not as bad as it seems."

She huffed. "I demand we stop at the next village we see." Sir Coulee and I bowed at her wishes and we all turned, beginning the small decline down toward the clearing. Every step I took

I reminded myself that it was that much closer to a physician. The pain in my arm burned fiercely and it was all I could do to focus on the path ahead.

I rested my good hand on my sword. The fingers tightened slightly around the hilt. I glanced back at her highness who was following without complaining. I looked back down at my hand.

A familiar spot.

Chapter 6

Sir Coulee led the way as I now took up the trail. The nobleman offered to lead an hour or so ago when I glanced at my wounded arm once again. It had bled through anew. I was slightly worried and I imagined the only reason he offered to go first was so that Princess Seattel would not keep seeing the cut. I took a sharp breath as we climbed over a fallen tree. I clenched my teeth.

"Is that not smoke?" the Princess asked, pointing into the valley before us. I followed her finger to a smoggy, gray gas climbing to the skies. Sir Coulee grinned and nodded, his dark brown hair bouncing.

"I believe so!"

Without more words, we began to walk in that direction. I was marveling at how well the Princess was doing with the exhausting trip. Waking up in fright, petrified as soldiers died in a gory fight before her, and watching in horror as one of her only friends was shot through the heart, and now fleeing the only place she knows. It was quite the horrific day. She did not say a word as we walked. She was quietly following the footsteps of the knight in front of her.

The birds chirped as the sun was now overhead, symbolizing it was close to noon. I wiped at the sweat dripping down my face. The trip was not as hard as others I have had before, however, I believed a fever was setting in because of my wound.

I was very relieved when the village came into sight. It was a fairly good size with children running and playing in the streets. There were a couple of vendors and a group of cow farmers chatting under the nearby trees. The entire village seemed to be surrounded by small farmlands and trees beyond that. We began to cross the newly planted fields.

The back of Princess Seattel's dress was full of mud and leaves. Multiple times we stopped as she was poked with sticks and twigs and I am sure that she will be stinging and sore for a few days. There was a stream a while back and I assisted her in cleaning the blood off her hands and her face. She helped me by ripping a piece of her dress as a bandage and Sir Coulee wrapped it for me.

I watched her closely as we walked and I know that she is close to breaking point. She kept the tears in, I am guessing for embarrassment of being caught sobbing by Sir Coulee, but kept her head high and posture as good as she could do. The horrific look on her face as Helen's blood washed downstream will be a memory I shall never forget.

"Perhaps it is best if we do not mention you are the Princess of the Evergreen," I pointed out to our group. "Better to lay low until we get down to the southern troops. After all, we do not know if anyone here is an ally to those brutes." The Princess agreed with me.

During the break at the stream we discussed where to flee to. Princess Seattel apparently was thinking the same as I. Our plan was drawn up to head down south to the army that was sent down there a few weeks before the Gems attacked in the Battle of the Ruby Tiger. Sir Coulee seemed quite upset; his attacks that sent the enemy running home did not scare them enough. They just attacked once again and with no resistance, apparently, and made it to the castle quick and easy enough.

Sir Coulee ran a hand through his dark hair and let the Princess take the lead. He spoke to me. "If these folks are friendly, I suggest staying for a few days so your arm can get the healing it needs."

"Hi!" a friendly voice called out, startling us out of our conversation and thoughts. "Welcome to our village, Thornwood!" We turned to the left, seeing a girl stand up from one of the fields. She waved at us, some mud flinging from her hands. She pushed back her blond hair and the mud streaked on her forehead. Wearing a straw hat to keep the spring sun out of her face, the girl approached. Her blue eyes scanned us.

Sir Coulee spoke politely to the girl. "Hello. We are hoping for a place to rest for the night." He glimpsed at her dirty dress before meeting her eyes once again. He gave a lopsided smile.

Her eyes twinkled. "But of course! We have no village inn unfortunately. Not too many strangers come through here. However, my beloved and I just finished an expansion on our house! Kenne! Come over here!" She waved over a sandy blond hair man. He was taller and tanner than she was, although she herself was way darker than the Princess. Even though it was only springtime, she obviously had her share of time in the sun. It was quite warm already.

The man approached and nodded at us. He was holding a pitchfork and had what I assumed was mud on his trousers. "Yes Olympia?" He raised an eyebrow while looking at the finer fabrics of Princess Seattel's dress. I narrowed my eyes slightly and my hand rested on the familiar spot.

The girl beamed at him. "These weary travelers have nowhere to rest and would like to stay the night in the village. Shall we offer our home?" The man stared a little longer, almost as if trying to piece together why a knight, a woman in finer clothes, and a gentleman such as myself were traveling together. I remembered the king's crest on my shoulder pads and made a quick note to myself to find a change of clothes. "Please...." the girl dragged out. Sir Coulee raised an eyebrow at the informal behavior but did not mention it.

The man must have been used to her, as he simply rolled his eyes at her pleads and folded his arms across his chest. "Fine. They can stay in the new additions." I let out a breath I did not know that I had in me and relaxed almost every muscle in my body. I did not realize I was that tense.

We were safe for the night. We had rooms.

The girl let out a squeal of excitement and grabbed Princess Seattel's arm in a friendly manner. The Princess was quite startled at getting touched, especially by a stranger. She glanced at me, slightly worried, but I just nodded subtly, informing her that the behavior was fine and that she would not be harmed by a simple grab from a farmer girl. Olympia was already chatting away, heading toward what I assume is her home. "This is great! We can test out the new rooms! They were finished last week and I just bought a blanket for the -'' Her voice trailed off as they walked out of hearing range and I felt my anxiety spike a little.

This was the farthest away I have been from the Princess for years.

"Hey." Kenne interrupted my thoughts. I tried to shove the panic deep inside of myself and I turned toward the man, my face emotionless. I threw a small smile his way, masking the amounts of nervousness I felt in my gut. His brown eyes locked onto my bleeding arm. "Would you like to follow me to the physicians?"

Sir Coulee stepped forward. "We would appreciate that." The sun was really hot. I swallowed and wiped away some more of the sweat dripping down my face.

The man nodded and turned away and in an instant my feet began walking in the direction that the Princess headed. Kenne stopped me. "This way." I ran a hand through my hair. My hair was sticky. I was so sure that the Princess had gone to the left, not the right.

I looked at the corner the Princess disappeared behind and then back to Kenne, who was standing with an eyebrow raised, as if expecting me to follow. My eyes darted to the corner once more. Kenne coughed. I could hear my heartbeat in my ears. I felt it in my stomach.

Sir Coulee pushed me a bit toward Kenne. "That arm has a bad cut, Washeen. You need a physician." The wind blew and the trees whispered as they bent to its will. I swallowed but my tongue seemed to get stuck in my mouth. I shuddered as the wind blew again, feeling the cold settle in my bones. Right. The physician.

I narrowed my eyes as Sir Coulee pushed once again. I planted my feet. "No. I do not need a physician." I needed to get to Princess Seattel. Was she safe? Where was she again? Did she not have reading classes in the library this time of day?

Sir Coulee glared back at me. "Do not be an idiot. You probably already have an infection. Look at your arm." I blinked at the knight. I was really tired. I looked at my arm that the knight was pointing too. There was blood on it. I got dizzy from looking down and I tried to catch my balance. Sir Coulee placed his hand on my shoulder.

"Why am I bleeding again?" His face swam in my vision before everything went black.

Chapter 7

I awoke with a cold sweat on my forehead. Shivering, I pulled up the sheet to my chin before letting out a groan of pain. It took a great deal of effort but I managed to look at the throbbing flesh. My lower left arm had a white bandage on it.

I narrowed my eyebrows and tried to sort through my fuzzy mind as I glanced around the room. There was a basket in the corner and in the opposite, a wooden table and chair. Which room in the castle was this? Why was my arm bandaged? The blanket smelled fresh and was quite crispy, I guessed from being dried in the wind.

Princess Seattel! I sat straight up, ignoring the burning pain flowing through the left side of my body. I stumbled forward and grabbed my sword that was placed neatly on the dresser. The strange room was lightened by a few candles placed strategically around.

I opened the door quickly and stepped into a bigger room with another bed. There were chemicals and plants sitting on tables and a few things brewing in different pots. Honestly, the air smelt so horrific I thought I would hurl. My eyes narrowed in on another door in the corner of the room and without hesitation I charged forward, blade in my right hand and a little shaky, but determined to find the Princess.

Outside was dark with a small breeze. I seemed to be in some sort of village, with houses to the right and left of me. The moon was bright and once again, I couldn't help but shake from the chill in the air.

"Oh my!" I whirled around and placed my sword blade against the neck of the voice that startled me. An older man raised his hands in innocence and I quickly lowered my weapon.Whether I looked confused or whether the old man was being polite, I do not know. He spoke in a rusty voice. "Hello! I am Belling, son of Ham. I am the physician of this fine village." He did a slight bow and I did one back. "I did not expect you to be awake yet. I had to treat your infection and thought you would have at least sleep a day. Will you please come inside so that I may inspect your wound once again?"

"No!" I pulled myself away from his poking fingers and slightly turned my body so that he could not see my arm. "I need to find the Princess first and ensure her safety."

The physician seemed startled. "The girl?" Then, surprisingly, let out a laugh. "You young folk never can listen. Well, hurry and check on her boy. She is in that house there." He pointed to a slightly bigger house down the pebbled path. The roof looked new and a candle flickered in a window that was open just a tad. "Come back in a little while so that I can check out that wound once again." The man nudged me with his cane before turning, heading into his own home.

I wasted not a moment and jogged to the house, throwing open the door. "Princess!" I frantically glanced around the shadowy room, registering a few faces, including Sir Coulee. And then, I saw her, sitting wrapped in a blanket on a wooden chair. She seemed quite shocked to see me.

"Sir Washeen?" She quickly stood and placed the blue blanket on the chair before heading over to where I stood in the doorway. "What are you doing up already? It has only been half a day! How is your wound?" She lightly touched my bandaged arm and I let out a small hiss.

"You should still be in bed," Sir Coulee frowned. His eyes flickered to us before he looked back toward the other two people in the room. The blond girl's jaw was dropped open and she looked flabbergasted. Eyes wide, she glanced at the man next to her before snapping back toward the Princess.

"Princess?!"

"Yes!" I snapped toward her, frustrated that the farmer girl did not know royalty when she saw it. "Princess Seattel of the _"

"That is enough!" Sir Coulee arose from his chair and glared in my direction. "Close your mouth, Sir Washeen, or have you forgotten what we spoke of in the woods?" His brown eyes seemed frozen as they pierced my own. I glared back, yet, I was confused. Woods? We were in the woods?

It all came rushing back to me. The warning bell, the fight, the chase, the woods, Helen... everything. I inhaled sharply and the Princess took a step back. "Oh. Right." I spoke softly. The room was quiet for a few seconds as the candles flickered comforting light all around. The fire crackled and Sir Coulee slowly sat back down in his chair, holding his hands to his head. His eyes met mine once again and I continued to hold my head high, refusing to acknowledge my mistake. An owl hooted in the distance.

The blond girl, who I now recognized as Olympia, spoke shakily once again. "Princess?" Kenne, next to her, shakily ran a hand through his hair.

The Princess smiled at the girl before her. "Do not worry. It is only a title. This does not change anything." She fixed her dress. I tried to stop my shaking arm as I placed my sword against the wall, next to the doorframe. It was obvious there was no danger present for now. Besides, I still had the dagger in my boot.

"This changes everything!" Olympia gushed, standing from her seat by the fire. She began pacing the hut. "You are staying in my house! This must seem like a pigpen compared to your palace." The girl frantically did a curtsy as she paced past the Princess. "I gave you seeds to feed the chickens!"

"It was the least I could do in thanks for your hospitality," the Princess softly laughed, folding her hands in front of her. She smiled at the pacing girl, obviously finding humor in this situation. I watched as Olympia tried to straighten her own clothing, now realizing she was in the presence of royalty.

"You did chores! You swept my floor-"

The Princess interrupted her small rant once again. "I asked what could be done to help you out." I raised my eyebrows in surprise. I could not believe Princess Seattel would sweep the floor of this house. I did not realize she knew how to even hold a broom. I scanned my memory. Has she ever even touched a rag or a cleaning cloth? I held back a smirk as I pictured the Princess poking the floor with the wrong end of a broom.

Olympia continued to do small curtsies in front of my grace. The Princess giggled as she placed a hand on the girl's arm. "Olympia, it is fine! I offered."

The farmer girl practically wailed. "But you cleaned my house! My dress must seem like rags to you!" The two girls bickered back and forth for a while as Princess Seattel continued to ensure it was fine and Olympia had a small breakdown. Between the ramblings, the Princess giggled, catching Sir Coulee's gaze. I narrowed my eyes as he smiled back. She flipped her hair over her shoulder and turned back to the farmer girl.

Sir Coulee interrupted the conversation by turning and talking toward Kenne. "Thank you again for opening up your home." I saw him hesitate as he looked around what was probably a hut to him. "Your addition is...adequate."

I winced at the harsh pleasantries coming from the knight's mouth. I narrowed my eyes. "Sir Coulee means to say, 'the addition is beautiful.'" I nodded my head toward the hallway with another room off the side. It was obvious that this part of the building was newer, with the wood fresh and the lumber smell present. There were some impressive designs carved into the beams.

Kenne nudged another piece of wood into the fire, making sparks fly around. He poked it with the fire stick before nodding his gratitude toward the noble knight. "Thank you. As the village leader, we sacrificed a lot of materials and precious time to expand our house."

"Why?" Sir Coulee questioned the man. I put myself down in a chair next to the knight. Sweat was beading on my face as I felt myself reach the end of the adrenaline rush. I gave a small smile to Olympia who offered me a jug of water. I drained the entire thing.

"You must explain," Kenne raised his glass toward the knight and myself, "why we are hosting our home to the Princess of the Evergreen. Not that it is not an honor," the man fumbled over his words and Olympia gave a nervous laugh. "It is a great honor. Just rather confusing." He picked at a sliver on his chair.

I narrowed my eyes once again at the change of topic as Kenne did not answer Sir Coulee's question. Meanwhile, Sir

Coulee leaned back in his chair, ignoring the topic change completely. Perhaps he did not even notice?

Olympia placed a blanket on my lap as I begged my weary body not to shake. I would not rest until I was sure the Princess was asleep. It was familiar, being beside her side before she woke and leaving right after she fell asleep. "It is a long story," Princess Seattel admitted. Ignoring the painful pull in my muscles, I pulled her chair closer to my side and she sat dainty, as usual, hands folded on her lap. Her dress looked scratchy and I could tell she was somewhat uncomfortable by the way she was sitting.

Nothing like those fine silks that she was used to.

Sir Coulee looked between myself and the Princess before tilting himself toward the village leader. He began to explain our adventures in great detail and I watched as the candle wick slowly began to die. I blinked heavily.

The Princess' dress was hanging to dry in the kitchen area and I watched as the final drops of water fell from it. Olympia sat forward in her chair, eyes sparkling at the adventures we had encountered. Princess Seattel was sitting stiff as Sir Coulee skipped over the death of the only girl she could possibly count as a friend. After all, he did not know that part of the story.

My eyes started to close but I forced them open. When I glanced up from my hands, Kenne was watching me. Our eyes met. "Perhaps it is time for bed," the man suggested, looking around the group. "It has been a long few days by the sounds of it."

"Your two's room is here," Olympia stood and waved her hand to one of the new rooms. "Sir Coulee you may sleep on some blankets in this main room. My eyes rested on the final doorway in the house, figuring it was Olympia and Kenne's chambers.

"Thank you," Princess Seattel spoke, strolling into the darkened room. I stood to follow. Kenne placed a metal sheet in front of the fire so that it would not accidently spread into the house. Olympia folded the small blanket that I had used and placed it on the ground for a pillow. Kenne bid us all a quick goodnight as well before ducking into his shared chambers, Olympia following.

Sir Coulee grabbed my right arm. I held in a grunt as the muscles seemed to stretch to my left arm's wound.

"I need to speak to you outside for a moment," the knight informed me. I glanced between the Princess in the room and the knight. It was not the first time that I had slept in the same room as Princess Seattel. Was Sir Coulee thinking it was somehow not right? I am, after all, her personal guard. Then, I paused. I am sure that Sir Coulee did not tell Olympia and Kenne that I was my highness' personal guard. Why did they assume I was to share a room with her?

My head snapped back to the conversation in front of me and the thoughts fled my head. "Can it not wait?"

"It cannot."

"I am the Princess' personal guard," I reminded the mistaken knight. "I have slept in the same room as her before."

Sir Coulee did something a nobleman rarely did. He rolled his eyes. "It is not about the rooms." I met his eyes once again. They were serious. Stern.

"Let us be quick about it then," I told the man before opening the door into the chilly night. He stepped out behind me and began to speak.

Chapter 8

"**A**s a knight, I expected more of you," Sir Coulee spoke, beginning to pace around in front of the house. "First, you barely escape the castle with the Princess. Second, you did not bring any supplies with you at all and next you even managed to catch yourself a nasty wound! The physician said you were dehydrated!" The knight kicked a rock and I watched as it skittered down the path. He lowered his voice, keeping his temper in control. "Why did you not have proper supplies ready in case this very thing happened?"

I narrowed my eyes. "I did not expect that the Gems would have enough stealth to ever cross our kingdom and invade the castle without us even hearing a rumor about it."

The brown hair knight raised an eyebrow at this. He turned to face me. "And your wound? Do you not have special training, being the guard of the only heiress of the kingdom? How is it that her personal guard could not protect himself from their blades?"

"My job is not to protect myself. My job is to protect my Princess." I folded my arms. "Not only was I battling against four men, but mistakes do happen. Princess Seattel remains unharmed." I refuse to tell him about Sir Chelan and Sir Everett. I ignored the flashback of the blade ripping into my skin as if it were ham. My arm throbbed.

"You cannot afford mistakes," Sir Coulee hissed at me as he turned to pace once again. "This is not some game. Her life is in danger, especially now."

I huffed in disbelief. The attitude of the man was getting under my skin, yet I refused to act on the negative feelings. "Do you think I do not know that?"

The man before me glowered. "I am suggesting that you act more responsible. As a knight, the Princess' life is my responsibility as well. As a pureblood, I believe I am more capable in defending it." Sir Coulee lifted his nose at me. I began to see a few more of his true colors. He was not as noble as he cared for people to think. But, I chose to ignore the last comment, shoving the small stinging feeling of insignificance it gave me deep down inside.

"Are you questioning my position?" I practically spat out. I clenched my teeth and glared at the nobleman, tone suggesting that he rethink his last statement.

"Precisely." He gave no heed to the warning in my voice. The knight, however, refused to meet my eyes and rested his vision beside me, onto the door of the house.

I straightened my posture and held a slight height advantage over my fellow knight in arms before me. Firmly, I stood my ground. "You have no right. The King himself appointed me as Guard of the Evergreen Princess and I refuse to let your words of doubt affect me. As the King spoke in the throne room during my knighting ceremony, 'Her skin will not feel any steel of any blade so long as your body has breath in it. If a life or death situation comes in play, you have authority over her, over any knight or nobleman, to secure her safety.'" I smirked toward Sir Coulee. "You fit in this category, as a knight AND as a nobleman, even as pureblooded as yourself. I am doing everything to insure her safety." I turned my back to the man and approached the front door.

"You fainted in the field today." His voice came off as strong but I could sense the doubt his mind plagued him with. My fingers touched the door handle.

"As you said, I was dehydrated. I lost a lot of blood. In my eyes, I still acquired Princess Seattel's safety in this village."

Sir Coulee scoffed. "And how did you know that this village is so safe for her?"

I waved my arms around the village before us. The moon was bright once again and outlined a few farmer huts on the horizon. A few torches on the path still flickered as the oil burned its last liquid up. Everything was quiet. "Does there seem to be danger nearby?"

There was a moment of silence before Sir Coulee spoke again. "You cannot just know that."

"They did not recognize her when they first met her," I reminded the knight, referring to Olympia and Kenne. My blood boiled at his tone of voice toward me and I inhaled another breath before speaking. "I took notice of their eyes and body language. Besides, why would they even begin to suspect that she is the Princess." I turned and slowly opened the door, careful not to let the wood creak and awake whoever was sleeping inside. "Have a good night, Sir Coulee."

Apparently Sir Coulee did not believe this conversation was over. His voice boomed behind me. "You told these peasants about her royal bloodline!"

"Good night, Sir Coulee." The knight's face was red but he could tell that the conversation was over. I spoke one last time. "And if these peasants are not to your liking, you may sleep outside."

I shut the door in his face with a click before exhaling an enormous breath that I did not know I had in me. Olympia stood in the kitchen with a clay mug and she gave me a small, comforting smile. How much of that conversation had she heard, I did not know. I looked up at the sound of a mug sliding along the wooden table. It came to a rest directly in front of me.

"Care for a drink?"

I smiled back at the cheery girl and pushed the mug back toward her. "No thank you. I will take you up on that offer another night." I bid her goodnight and with a small nod back, I reached for my sword resting by the doorframe and then headed down the hall toward the wooden door that separated our room from the rest of the house.

Princess Seattel was settled in the bed already, covered in a wool blanket. Her dress was draped over the wooden chair in the corner and I could see her nightgown covered shoulder poking out from under the covers. I carefully removed the green dress and placed it on the small bedside table, swapping it with another blanket. My sword was placed against the wall. I settled down for the night, resting my feet on the wooden chest to my left.

I looked around the room. There was a small candle flickering with a short wick, not going to last more than a few moments longer. There were some pegs in the wall next to the door for hanging some coats on and the window beside that was perfectly aligned with the beams going across the roof. I marveled for a second at how well done this room was built and wondered exactly how this couple could afford it. Kenne did mention that he was village leader, so he must have saved up for a while. Princess Seattel's deep breaths were a soothing background noise.

The candle had one last wink before it casted me into darkness. It took a second for my eyes to adjust as the moon cast a glow across the room. My eyelids were weighted. I drifted off to sleep.

-=--=-=--=- Guard of the Evergreen Princess -=--=-=--=-

A shriek woke me up. Blinking my sleep away in a second, my hand was grasping my sword and I had leaped myself onto the Princess' bed. She was sitting straight up. "Get down!" I growled at her. I aimed my blade toward the door.

It took a few moments, the door not moving an inch, before I realized it was the Princess that had yelled out. "Sir Washeen." There were tears in her voice and quickly I stepped off the bed and sat down next to the black haired lady, her bottom lip quivering. The tears on her cheeks alerted me to a possible nightmare.

The door burst open and Sir Coulee barged in with his sword raised. Princess Seattel let out a squeak and tried to cover herself with the wool blanket. After all, she was only in a night-gown.

"Get out!" I hissed at the man in front of me. He seemed to ignore me completely and gazed around the room. I could feel the uncomfortableness radiating off of the heiress beside me.

"Princess. Is everything okay?" He began to approach the bed. I glanced to my left and saw the Princess shielding away from the man in front of her. I placed myself between his line of sight and Princess Seattel. She let out another small sob sound and placed her shaky hand on my back. I tensed up.

"Leave us, Coulee."

"I am checking to see if the-"

"Leave." The disrespect that the knight was showing was unacceptable. I stared the man down. "Now."

With that simple word and a final look, Sir Coulee left the room slowly, shutting the door quite loudly on his way out. I focused my attention on the distraught Princess, cursing myself that I had not thought of her having a bad dream. After all, she had witnessed a great deal of people die before her. "Princess?"

The salty water drops began flowing down her cheeks as she threw her legs over the side of the bed and sat along next to me. There were some sniffles and she wiped away the water with her hands. Her black hair was quite tangled and symbolized a restless,uneasy sleep.

The house fell into quiet once again as Sir Coulee seemed to stop his stomping and return to his bed. We sat there for quite a long moment, myself listening for any more cues of distress, herself trying to calm down.

Only the sound of quiet hiccups echoed in the room. Then slowly, she moved her hand to my arm and rested it on my elbow. The tips of her fingers paused on the bandage above my wound before staying there. I held my breath at the delicate touch. "It was just a terrible dream." I expected as much.

"About Helen?"

She nodded, sniffling. Her blue eyes looked into mine. I almost broke my professional posture as the glassy tears began to fall once again. She started to say something once again but her voice broke. With a little more effort, she managed to speak. It was almost a whisper. "She is dead, is she not?" It was more of a statement than anything.

"Yes, my Princess." Her body shook once more as silent tears rolled down her face. Witnessing a friend's death is no small thing, especially if it is not expected. My line of work required me to push past those feelings. I was fine. I was unaffected. I had seen death.

I was fine.

My thoughts were disturbed as the Princess let out another sob. Her hand tightened on my arm. She laid her head on my shoulder and her black hair fell in waves behind. Never before had she done this. But then again, previously, there was always Helen.

Slowly, I moved my arm from her grasp. She lifted her head a tiny bit and blinked at me. I debated for a moment before I repositioned my arm behind her back and around her side. Comforting someone was not a skill that I mastered, let alone even had. With her sigh of satisfaction, I figured I was on the right track. I pulled her a bit closer. My hand rested on the silky touch of the nightgown. Laying her head back down onto my shoulder she sniffled quietly into my ear.

"Thank you, Washeen."

I swallowed the urge to answer with the unusual formalities. "You are welcome, Princess Seattel."

Chapter 9

My eyes snapped open as I heard a slight bang sound coming from the kitchen. I recognized it as metal on metal, specifically a pot or pan. Next, some humming moved throughout the house. Somehow, during the Princess' dream and the rest of the night, we ended up laying on the bed, her head still on my shoulder.

I gently moved Princess Seattel off my shoulder and onto the pillow and her hair fanned out across it. Then, I quietly got off the mattress, opened the door, and closed it softly. I stretched. The night seemed longer as I was woken up halfway through. I still received a decent sleep, however my back was a little stiff.

The morning was cold and chilly but no candles were needed as the sun was already bright outside the window. Olympia gave Kenne a peck on the cheek before he turned and went out the front door, shovel in hand. Sir Coulee let out a snore from his bed on the floor.

"Good morning," Olympia smiled brightly at me as she rubbed the sleep out of her eyes. She went around to the kitchen and clattered some more pans out of the cupboard. My stomach growled and I realized I had not eaten since two days before. Suddenly, I could not wait to dine. "Sleep well?"

"Yes." I watched as she scurried about. "Thank you for opening your house for us."

Olympia beamed. "It is no problem." She scanned the kitchen and the pile of dishes from their supper the day before. "Would you like to help get breakfast ready?" She poked some of the coals on the cooking fire. I nodded at her.

"Would you like me to cook or clean?"

"If you could stir the oatmeal that would be great!" She gave me a wooden spoon and I began to stir the food in front of me, swallowing and forcing myself not to quickly take a bite whilst she was turned. Some chickens clucked outside.

Last night, as the Princess snoozed on my shoulder, I realized a few things. First, Sir Coulee is a little more stuck up than I had first anticipated. The pureblood comments had not come out of nowhere.

Olympia let out a yawn and I glanced at the girl before looking down once more to the brownish food in front of me. Children giggled outside.

The way Sir Coulee scanned over the village, over Kenne and Olympia when he first arrived, as if they were dirty and could not be trusted, showed signs of either being spoiled as a child or being born with a silver spoon in his mouth. The comment that Sir Coulee made about the addition in this house now boiled my blood. This house was the biggest one in the village and it must have cost the couple quite a lot of coin. We were also the first to stay in the new room and I felt honored about that.

Speaking of the man, there was a creak from the floor as he arose from his makeshift bed. Breakfast smelled amazing and I have no doubt that the aroma is what awoke him. He stretched and I watched as he approached Olympia. "When will breakfast be ready?"

"Good morning, Coulee," the girl spoke without turning from her spot by the sink. "Did you sleep well?" I inwardly smirked. She had forgotten the nobleman's title and I could tell by Sir Coulee's body language that it irked him so. Knowing that Olympia was not used to such manners, I tried to step in helpfully. The knight spoke first, however.

"Adequately." I narrowed my eyes as the word was spoken harshly.

"Would you like to help Kenne with the morning chores? I believe all he has left is to collect the eggs from the hen. He can show you the chicken coup."

"No thank-"

"KENNE!" A voice I never knew a woman had erupted from this girl's lungs. "May you show Coulee the chicken coup?" Sir Coulee's eyes were wide as he stared in shock at the unladylike behavior happening in front of him.

I stifled a laugh. This moment was quickly over, however, when Princess Seattel emerged from the bedroom, rubbing her head.

"Headache, Princess?" I asked her, approaching her quickly. I forced myself not to brush back a piece of black hair from her face and instead, looked into her sleepy eyes. My hand continued to rest on the hilt of my sword.

She waved me off with her hand and then ran it through her black hair, fixing the funky piece. "I am fine. I just had a strange sleep." I backed off slowly, double checking her out of the corner of my eye, before heading back to the oatmeal. Kenne came in from outside and held the door open. Sir Coulee, without knowing how to say no, followed the man outside. Olympia came to the pot and glanced into it.

"Looks finished to me." She motioned to a chair and the Princess took a seat as her breakfast was placed before her. Oatmeal and a hard boiled egg.

"I do not need this. You eat it." She tried to give it back, as the way Olympia had handed it to her demonstrated how rare an egg like that was for breakfast, but the cheery girl refused.

"I would like you to eat it! We usually sell them in the market for coin but today is a special day! It is not very often that we get to host a Princess!" She bustled around the kitchen, but kept a close eye on the royal lady, making sure the egg was cooked to perfection as she took her first bite. I began to shovel down the oatmeal, forgetting how wonderful it tasted.

Kenne opened the door and wandered in, followed by Sir Coulee, who was carrying a small basket with two more eggs. Kenne smelled the air, sighing deeply. He took his place without a word and began to eat. I watched as Sir Coulee eyed the egg sitting on my Princess' plate.

His plate did not have one.

-=--=-=--=- Guard of the Evergreen Princess -=--=-=--=-

A few hours later Princess Seattel and I were settled in the shade underneath a tree as we watched a few of the village farmers work in their fields. I had visited the physician once again and Belling made a huge deal about how I did not come back later that night. I scowled as he also spoke rudely to the Princess, who in his mind had forgotten to send me back. The Princess took the scolding surprisingly well, apologizing to the man and acknowledging that my infection could have gotten worse. I tried to step in and blame myself but Belling was stubborn.

My arm now supported a new bandage. It felt increasingly better and did not ache as it did last night. There was a slight burning pain but Belling said it was the medicine fighting the infection. I watched as the men worked tirelessly in the fields before me, itching to help with the heavy load. Belling, however, would not let me help with farm chores.

"This life seems so peaceful compared to the castle." Princess Seattel picked a blade of grass from the ground in her cross-legged position. I watched the Princess carefully, noting how relaxed she looked. Here she did not need to mind her manners as much and did not have servants and nobles watching her every movement. "There are no busy servants running here and there, no men watching my every move," she voiced my thoughts. She sat perfectly straight, however, and gracefully pulled back a piece of her hair that was in her face. "I feel truly relaxed."

I nodded at her as she turned and met my brown eyes with her crystal blue ones. "It is nice."

"How long are we staying here for?" the Princess inquired. She glanced around the village and I noticed how her gaze rested on Sir Coulee, stretched out and laying against another tree farther down the stone path. He was not snoozing, but was watching a few of the women work in the raspberry plants. They were giggling to themselves, knowing that a handsome stranger was watching them. Every so often, though, the knight glanced at the Princess before noting I was still there keeping watch over her.

As if I would leave her.

"I suggest we continue our path towards the south tomorrow morning for sure," I gave her my input. "The castle must be overrun otherwise the king would have sent messengers to the villages, searching for you." I took a moment before I continued to talk, taking note of how her gaze did not move from the knight. "When we make it to the south and reconnect with the army down there, we can fight our way back toward the castle and claim back what is rightfully yours." I ran my fingers around the hilt of my sword sitting on my hip. A battle was not a place I wanted to be but if that was the only way to get Princess Seattel back on the throne, then I would fight tooth and nail.

Princess Seattel turned my way. "Is your arm going to be ready for more traveling, Sir Washeen?"

I smirked at her. "Since when do you use your arm for walking?" I watched as laughter filled her features and the sound filled the air around us.

"Fair point. I fear it may be too soon, however." She gently touched the bandage.

"The sooner we make it down south, the better, your grace," I firmly nod at the lady beside me. She looked down and fiddled with a blade of grass before nervously looking back up at me. Her eyes darted from me to the figure of Olympia, bending over and weeding a patch of strawberries. She took a quick peek towards the knight once again.

"Sir Washeen, is my father still alive?"

"For sure." I erased all of the doubt in the Princess' mind, refusing to let her pounder over such upsetting things. Once again, the Princess spoke.

"Sir Washeen, can I speak honestly?"

"Of course, Princess!" I shifted myself closer, showing her that I was ready to listen to what she had to say. The blade of grass in her hands was in shreds but she skillfully managed to weave it together. I could tell that all those lessons in needle-work paid off.

Princess Seattel looked up at me. "Can we not call each other by first names? I fear these titles will end us in trouble if we need to stop the habit suddenly. Such as last night." There was a twinkle in her eyes, showing that she was not upset that Olympia and Kenne learned her secret. I understood what she was saying however, knowing that we cannot trust others as quickly as these villagers. We also do not want slip ups if we run into more serious places, conversations, or areas.

I contemplated my answer. "If I say yes, what shall I call you, Princess?"

She smiled toward me as Olympia stepped foot on the path and headed our way. She had a floppy hat on, not that it was doing any good as her cheeks were tinged red from the sun already. Princess Seattel's voice was soft as the girl approached. "What about just my name?"

I gulped but before I could answer, Olympia began to speak. "Hey Seattel! Washeen." I nodded her way. "That Coulee sure loves impressing the ladies!" she observed, watching the knight subtly flex as he picked up his sword off the grass. I narrowed my eyes, hating the way he wasted his energy fooling around when he easily could be helping Kenne with chores, a fair payment for our stay.

A small movement of the Princess caused my focus to lie on her once again. Could I call Princess Seattel by her first name without it being awkward? For years, she has been 'Princess'. Last night was a different story. Last night was the one and only time that would happen. She needed friendship. Helen was not there.

"That is for sure." Princess Seattel nodded firmly in agreement with the farmer girl, although she threw a glance at the knight once again. I narrowed my eyes. That was the third time.

The farmer girl sighed, before lifting her suntanned shoulders once more. She heaved the basket of raspberries back to her hip before turning. "Well, I am off to refill the indoor firewood stack!" She began tromping through the taller grass.

Princess Seattel suddenly sat up. "Olympia!" she called out to the girl. Olympia turned. Princess Seattel looked at me. "Would you like help? Washeen and I would not mind."

A smile stretched over the girl's face. "Of course! If you do not mind, that is," she hastendly added.

"We do not."

I stood first, offering my good hand to Princess Seattel before me. She took it and gracefully stood, wiping the blades of grass from her lap. "Thank you, Washeen." She straightened her dress.

I met her crystal eyes. "You are welcome... Princess."

Chapter 10

"Where is Kenne?" Olympia pondered mainly to herself. She busied herself around the kitchen, every now and then glancing out of the window. Princess Seattel was currently chopping some food for dinner and Sir Coulee was sharpening his sword. The two had spent a while together before dinner and it boiled my blood knowing that Sir Coulee could make her laugh so hard she received hiccups. Apparently they had enjoyed themselves.

I narrowed my eyes as she fluttered her eyes toward the man sitting in the wooden chair, especially when the man flexed harder as he moved his arms. I rolled my eyes. A small blush was on her cheeks. Olympia interrupted my thoughts. "Seriously! He is never this late for dinner!"

"I am sure he will be here soon." Princess Seattel tried to comfort the obviously upset girl. Olympia wrung her hands and looked out of the window once more, the sky darkening to a blue.

Sir Coulee arose from his chair. "Perhaps he is doing some last minute tasks?"

"There was nothing left to do!" Olympia practically wailed. Sir Coulee flinched at the loud female. I was surprised to see the girl this upset as I hadn't witnessed a smile off her face before. "We had stocked the fire wood and I had even drawn fresh water for tomorrow morning!" The Princess sent a compassionate look toward the girl and helpfully stirred the supper.

A thought crossed my mind and before I could think it through, Sir Coulee began to approach Princess Seattel. I blurted it out, slightly distracted at the action of the knight. "Perhaps Sir Coulee and I could go look for him?" Sir Coulee sent me a glare but the damage was done. I knew that this was the last thing he wanted to do. Olympia was beyond overjoyed that we would help her.

"You would do that for me?"

Sir Coulee took this moment to flaunt his lifestyle choice. "Of course. I am a knight. We could never leave a damsel in distress." I watched as his eyes flickered toward Princess Seattel, who looked happily beyond happy at the 'knight in shining armor.' I held back the many sharp comments I felt the need to speak and instead decided to nod at Olympia before making my way out of the door. Sir Coulee followed. Once the door was shut, the knight hissed at me.

"What were you thinking?"

"Whatever do you mean?"

He snorted, not using any noble manners whatsoever. "Why would you volunteer us for this pointless mission? Kenne is obviously going to wander back to his home by himself. He is probably at the pub." Our boots crackled on the stone path as we headed deeper into the village.

I double checked the knight to make sure he was not joking with me. He was serious. "I do not think that Kenne is the pub type." I swear I have only heard that man speak a handful of times since we were here and I could not picture him drinking the night away with strangers.

"He has the money for it," Sir Coulee insisted. "Look at their house. Is it not suspicious that they recently did an addition to the building?" He moved his arms toward the other buildings in town. "The rooms in his house are massive and decorated beautifully. This town is not that big. They should not be able to afford what they do." I scratched the top of my head and sighed, watching as one of the torches on the road was blown out by the wind. "Besides, there is more to do at the pub than simply drink."

"He did mention he was the village leader."

Sir Coulee snorted once more and startled, I looked over at the knight, confused at why he would act in such a common manner. "He is not drinking. Village leaders do not usually have that much coin. I would know as I have been to dozens of villages in my travels." His nose tipped upward.

"Perhaps they had been saving their coin?"

"They are young," the knight pointed out and I raised my eyebrows, realizing that he did make a good point. "Unless they have had a family member pass and they inherited coin that way, I do not think it would be possible." Sir Coulee kicked a rock down the path. "By the looks of this village, not many people have much coin." I glanced around at the houses that we have passed, shocked that the knight was once again right. I guess I have not been paying full attention.

Sir Coulee continued to talk as I saw the pub sign in the distance. "I believe Kenne is doing under the table tasks." The man held his head higher and ran a hand through his brown hair.

My eyes widened. "You mean smuggling?!"

Sir Coulee scoffed toward me. "Do not sound so surprised. It happens a lot." This fact flabbergasted me. I guess Sir Coulee was more experienced with this sort of situation. After all, he has traveled his entire life. I glanced at the man out of the corner of my eye as we walked the final steps.

Sir Coulee halted in front of the wooden door. I could hear laughter inside and smelled liquor, sweat, and some sort of stew. All in all, mixed together, there was a horrible smell emitting from the building. "When we go in, follow me to the back corner. If Kenne is in here, he will be up to something." I nodded at the knight and with that assurance, Sir Coulee opened the door and walked instantly to the left. I followed.

It was a basic pub inside. There was a main counter with the liquors and men at some of the tables. Some were playing games with dice and others were just enjoying a mug or two. Sir Coulee sat us at a table in the corner and nodded toward the left. I turned that direction. There was Kenne, facing away from us and seated with two other men.

Sir Coulee and I exchanged a look, knowing instantly that this was not good. Sir Coulee waved the barmaid away before she could approach any farther and blow our cover, as Kenne had not seen us yet. Even though there was a lot of chatter and loud belly laughs coming from nearby tables, we were just close enough to hear the conversation a few tables over.

Kenne raised his voice just a little. "You said you would give me fifty coin! This is only forty-three." One of the brutes across the way narrowed his eyes at the village leader. He was rough looking with a ripped black long coat and a colorful fabric piece wrapped around his forehead. His white shirt had a giant brown stain on the side and I hoped that it was mead.

"Be grateful you peasant!" The man glared at Kenne. "This is probably more money than you have seen in your meaningless life!" The last part of the sentence was spat.

Kenne folded his arms and raised his nose. "I am Village Leader. I have seen our treasury. This is nothing." However, his actions betrayed his words as he pulled the small leather sack closer to himself. He recounted the money.

"Now," the other Gem growled. "You said you know where the Princess is." Every nerve in my body went into shock and I could feel the blood pounding throughout my body. Next to me, Sir Coulee tensed up. He put his hand on the hilt of his sword and I placed my hand on mine. A familiar spot.

The black coated Gem slammed his fist on the table and Kenne's drink bounced. The blond haired man sat back slightly and I could tell by his body language he was a bit startled at the brutishness of the men. Most likely, this was more than he bargained for. The Gem threw another coin on the table and Kenne stuttered. "S-she's staying in my house with myself and my beloved." He reached for the coin greedily.

In an instant both men were up. One man had placed his hands on Kenne's hands, trapping him to the table by strength. He barked at the other man. "To his house! Quick! Kill everyone inside." His eyes glinted in the lanterned light of the tavern. "We want the Princess alive," he sneered.

"No!" Kenne's yell was desperate and he tried to get out of the black jacket Gem's hold. "Please! My beloved is home!" He pulled and twisted his wrists but the Gem had a deadly hold on them. The cup spilt and liquid sloshed on the floor.

"I do not give a mandrake root about your ronyon beloved," he snarled. He gave a look to his comrade and the second Gem rushed off. Nobody in the bar blinked as the man stormed out the door.

"Go!" Sir Coulee yelled at me. He grasped his sword and yanked it from his sheath, the metallic squeal alerting the remaining Gem to the Evergreen knight. I threw open the wooden door and frantically scanned the darkened streets for the Gem. My entire body tensed up when I saw him. The man was running down the path, shoving an elderly man out of the way. He was heading directly to Olympia and Kenne's house. Either he has been here before or the village leader's house is more obvious looking than I first realized.

I took off running, my feet barely touching the ground. One thought flew through my mind faster than the wind through my hair.

I had to get to the house first.

The man did not know that I was chasing him. I darted down a nearby yard and jumped over a wooden fence. A dog barked. There was some laughter coming from a nearby lightened window. My eyes rested on the house up ahead and instead of heading toward the front door, I leaped into the bedroom window, crashing onto the bed in the room. I almost tore the door of the hinges as I darted into the main room. Olympia and Seattel were settled on the floor by the fire, a few needles sitting around. A beautiful quilt was spread across their laps and both ladies were startled at the noise and the entrance that I took.

"Gems are coming!" I roared, unsheathing my sword and snagging my arm through the Princess'. She gasped and the color evaded from her face, leaving her hair looking blacker than ever. Olympia stood quickly as I began to lead Princess Seattel toward the door.

"Where are you going?"

"Anywhere but here!" I hissed at the girl. Princess Seattel was shaking on my arm and I blew out the candle that was on the table. We were plunged into almost complete darkness, except for the dim flickering that the dying fire was giving. A pounding knock interrupted my next sentence. I shoved the Princess behind me.

Without moving and creating sound on the creaking floor, I motioned for Olympia to get down and the girl hid behind the chair, tucking her knees under her chin. She folded the quilt over herself. The knocking continued and I shoved the Princess under the table between the chairs, placing myself by the door. When the door opens, I will be behind it.

My hand rested on the hilt of my sword. A familiar spot.

Chapter 11

Clearly having lost his patience, the Gem Warrior slammed his full weight against the flimsy wooden door of the house. With an ominous cracking, sending splinters of wood and a shattered hinge in my direction, the door fell to the floor and sent dust up in the air. I forced myself not to cough.

As the dust cleared, I saw an enormous Gem warrior standing in the doorway. He stood almost two heads taller than myself, and was stooping slightly in order to see into the doorway. His grayish-black beard was stained with ale and crumbs of food, and his mouth was twisted into a beastly snarl, revealing several broken and yellowed teeth. His muscled, heavily scarred arms flexed as he saw me standing there, my hand clenching the hilt of my sword. In his hand he held a gore-encrusted war axe, clearly never having cleaned the remains of any of his opponents off the blade save to sharpen it.

His face contorted into a vicious grin when he realized that I was not some simple peasant. A shiver ran down my spine as the Gem spoke in a guttural tone. I had never shared words with a Gem before. "And here I thought this would be an easy, pointless killing. I'm going to enjoy this!" His sentence turned into a ghastly roar at the last phrase, and he charged through the door and straight at me.

As a man of honor, I hadn't drawn my sword yet, foolishly expecting that the Gem would have given me the chance. I jumped aside from his charge, wheeling on my heels to keep him in my field of view. He swung his axe wide in my direction, and I ducked below the swing, lashing out with a fist into his gut. His abdomen was hard and muscular, and my fist seemed to have no effect on him. With his left hand, he took hold of my shoulder and flung me sideways across the room. I slammed into the table where Princess Seattel was hiding, feeling the pain of the table edge bludgeon into my side. The Princess shrieked in terror. In the spare moment I had, I drew my sword. Perhaps we'd be on equal footing now.

The Gem Warrior lunged at me again, swinging his axe wildly. Using an oft-practiced maneuver of my sword, I dislodged the axe from his hands and used his own momentum to slam his upper body onto the table. Without hesitation, I took hold of his hair-matted head with my free hand, slamming his face into the surface of the table. The cartilage broke under the impact. The Princess screamed again as the table shuddered from the impact and several of the clay vessels slid off the table and onto the floor. With a shout the Gem broke free, using both his hands to seize me by the shoulders and slam his forehead into my jaw. I staggered backward from the shock of the blow, feeling the warm blood rush from my lip. I really dislike a split lip.

Swinging low, I lashed out with my sword at the Gem's leg. He grabbed my arm mid swing and squeezed hard. I felt my muscles bruise and crush under his grasp and I am sure my bones creaked ominously under the pressure. My hand dropped my sword, and it clattered onto the floor. I lunged forward toward my fallen lifeline, the Gem's grip still on my arm, and we both tumbled to the floor in front of the hearth. The fire was blazing hot. I rolled with the Gem warrior until we were closer to the fire sill, feeling the singing heat of the flames on my hair. The Gem warrior shouted in pain as I wrestled my arm free and shoved his hand and wrist into the fireplace. The heat was almost unbearable for me as I watched his hand crisp and burn like a roast duck.

The Gem warrior took advantage of my distraction to grab me by the throat with his other hand, shoving my head towards the fire in the hearth. He roared. The flames licked greedily at my hair, and I rolled away in desperation, letting his burning hand go free. I snatched a burning log that had been half sticking out of the fire and rolling to my feet, I swung the log downwards on the Gem's head as he was struggling to stand. I bashed his skull with burning wood. Chunks of burnt wood, ash, and cinders sprayed across the floor as I swung the log into his head several more times. The Gem collapsed onto the floor, writhing in pain.

Quickly, I reached for the knife in my boot, and, unsheathing it, I plunged it into his chest. The Gem warrior gasped, and his bloodshot eyes locked with mine for just a moment. He laughed an awful, gurgling laugh. Then, the Gem laid lifeless on the floor.

I ran a hand through my hair, frowning at the feeling. My hair was singed from the flames of the hearth. Struggling over to the Gem's lifeless body, I wrenched my knife out of his chest, wiping it off on his fur vest before sheathing it again. Slowly, I made my way over to my sword, also sheathing it as I shakily stood to my feet. My arm's joint ached, as the pain of the crushing grasp still whirled through it. The old wound has not seemed to open, which I counted as another victory.

I turned toward where the Princess was, underneath the wooden table, now with a bit of blood on it. "Let us go quickly before the second brute comes!" I was not sure if Sir Coulee had defeated the man or not.

"What about me?" I whirled around at the voice, sliding my sword out of the sheath and placing it in the air, in the direction toward the voice. Olympia stood in front of me now and I blinked, totally forgetting that the girl was there. She was looking at the distorted body that now littered her floor. Those stains would not be coming out easily.

Princess Seattel placed her hand on my arm and I looked at her. "She must come with us."

I shook my head. "She will only slow us down."

"She clearly is not safe here." The Princess gestured toward the body on the floor and my eyes darted toward the now splintered front door. I heaved a sigh. "Please Washeen!" I glanced at Olympia one more time, her face determined, yet her eyes teary. "I order you." My eyes met the Princess' crystal blue ones and I could tell she was stubborn in her answer.

"Fine. But we must go now." I was firm on my answer. Princess Seattel nodded her approval while Olympia scribbled a note on the table. Next, she snatched a bag from a hanger on the wall and began shoving her quilt and potatoes into the bag. I grabbed the Princess' arm and began walking toward the door. "Now means now!"

"But what about Kenne?"

"Are you coming?" I hissed back.

I heard the blond girl's footsteps race across the floor before I darted out into the night. It was darker than before and only a few torches along the path remained lit.

I headed south, turning the corner of the house before running straight into a darkened figure. In an instant, my sword was at his throat, pinning him against the wooden siding. One small movement and he would be a dead man.

"Seriously Sir Washeen?" the voice coughed out. "We must stop meeting this way."

"Sir Coulee!" Princess Seattel darted forward and pushed my sword arm down before I could even react. She stood before the man who wheezed slightly, out of breath for either he was running or I startled him severely. "Are you alright?"

The man straightened himself and fixed his cuirass, stepping into the sight of the torches. He was smirking slightly at the lady in front of him. "Quite, your highness." I noticed how his sword had a tinge of red, darker than his flushed cheeks. He was obviously embarrassed, having been taken by surprise and pinned to a building in front of the Princess. There was a cloth wrapped around his wrist, his hands were bloody, and a small slice was on his ear. Either he ducked too late or a stab was a little close for comfort. However, the man seemed to stand fine.

I wasted no time in getting information. "Did you stop the other Gem?" The wind blew a cold gust and I shuddered off a shiver.

The knight before me nodded. "Him and one other. Young, easy enough to finish off quickly." His eyes darted down the path and his face was stony once again. "There was mention from the young one about some sort of group coming to the village in a few moments. We really should get moving."

"Which direction?"

"I do not know."

"Right!" I turned sharply and began marching south, toward the forest line. "South is our best direction to go then." Princess

Seattel fell in step on my right side, Olympia following her and Sir Coulee taking up the tail. The grass blew against our legs and I was thankful that Olympia had given Princess Seattel a thicker blue dress. She also wore a shawl as well which I recognized as one Olympia had worn earlier.

There were small whisperings behind the Princess and myself. "Where is Kenne?" I glanced over my shoulder and saw Olympia, who had fallen in step with the knight. "Did you manage to find him before the Gems came?" The knight kept walking, at first ignoring the girl. A few moments went by before the girl asked again. I shot another look behind me and Sir Coulee had clenched his jaw.

I realized that nothing good would come from ignoring the questions. "I am sure Kenne is fine," I assured the girl behind me. "You, however, are in danger as the Gems know where you live."

"How do they know that?" the innocent girl asked. My feet crunched on some sticks and I made a mental note to be more aware of where I was placing my feet. We were entering the woods now, an owl's hoot echoing over the green trees and into the darkened branches. It was quite eerie, especially knowing there could be Gems beyond our steps.

"They must have been scouting our location." I gave an answer to her question, although I know it was the wrong one. The worst would be if she knew the truth and decided to turn around and go find Kenne herself.

"I hope he is fine. I left a note on the table so he will know where I went."

Kenne is dead. There is no doubt in that. Sir Coulee would have brought the man back if he could have. He would have left him and Olympia in their house. Was I happy that the traitor was no longer with us? Yes. But at the same time, I believe death was an extreme punishment.

We walked in silence for a while, leaving Thornwood farther and farther behind. A few times I had taken out my sword to hack at a few stray blackberry branches and one or two times stopped to help the girls over a fallen tree. Olympia, however, never needed the help and flawlessly slid herself over the bark. It showed that the girl had grown up in these woods. At least she would not slow us down.

It was about an hour later I glanced left and right across a path that we stumbled upon. It did not seem to be a very traveled path. No branches were broken and no footprints lined the small mud piles. I began walking down the dirt path, crushing the grass underneath my boots. Princess Seattel had paused and took up her walk next to Olympia. They were chatting softly about mindless things. The Princess had seemed to take quite a liking to the girl and I wondered if it was possibly a Helen rebound. I hope the friendship will last.

I was quite impressed with how well Princess Seattel was taking this whole new lifestyle. She was not your typical stuck-up royal, but at the same time she really appreciated her soaps and baths. I figured she knew there was no choice for her but to live this way.

I went back to thinking about our plan of making it to the south. Should we stop at more villages? Is that a bigger or smaller risk than just continuing through the woods? I sighed as questions flew through my head and I placed my hand on the hilt of my sword.

Chapter 12

It was many moments later before we stopped. We stood on the edge of a small cliff, a river flowed before us and with a quick look up and down the rushing water, it was apparent that the only way across would be a boat, a shallow section farther along, or a very rough and probably impossible swim. Sir Coulee and I began to discuss our next steps while the ladies went down the rocky waterfront.

"We should follow the water." Sir Coulee pointed down the stream and I followed his finger. The water did flow to the south and eventually we would need to cross in order to get to the troops.

"How did you cross in your other travels?" I questioned the man before me. I knew since he had gone on many quests and adventures he would know things about this land that I would not. The sun was now high in the sky and I estimated it was around midday.

Sir Coulee stretched his arms out, stretching his shoulders. "There was a town called Lone Pine and they had a shallower

part of the river. One could pay another to sail across the water." The man watched the ladies drink from the river before
placing the water canteen under the water. "However, that
town lies north of here." He pointed once again, this time upstream.

"So we would have to backtrack a bit," I caught on. My eyes
narrowed as Princess Seattel seemed to slip on a rock and
Olympia caught her arm. Both started giggling and I relaxed.
Olympia took off her shoes and placed her bare feet in the
water while Princess Seattel nobly folded her hands in front
of her and watched. I turned back toward Sir Coulee. "Is that
the smartest move? Is there not another town farther down the
river?" I ran a hand through my hair. "I wish we had some sort
of map."

"I do not know."

I nodded slowly. "Then we should head back upstream. It
appears to be our best option." I did not want to travel the
opposite direction, but it was better than following the river
downwards only to find out later on that Lone Pine is the only
place to cross. I wiped some of the sweat off my brow as the sun
continued to beat down on us. Moving throughout the forest
was no easy task as we were not following trails.

Sir Coulee motioned toward the women and began heading down the rocks. I followed his signal. Princess Seattel was
watching as Olympia tossed a few stones into the water. "We
make camp here for tonight," I said to the Princess and the

farmer girl as I scouted out the small rocky beach. The Princess looked a bit confused as she glanced toward the sky but I could tell she was weary from traveling all night. She did not say anything but nodded toward me.

Sir Coulee had caught a rabbit for dinner and Olympia was prepping it to eat. She opened up the pack that Sir Coulee had gentlemanly offered to carry for her, and pulled out a few potatoes.

This shocked Sir Coulee. "I was carrying potatoes around for half a day?"

"It was all that I had time to pack!" Olympia defended herself. The knight huffed but left the conversation alone, only throwing a nasty glare at the bag.

After skinning the animal and showing Princess Seattel the gutsy parts, the farmer girl chopped up a few plants that she had found in the woods and began making a delicious smelling stew. She also threw in a few potatoes. I had moved two bigger parts of a fallen tree into a small grassy clearing around the firepit that Sir Coulee had made. Princess Seattel had taken a seat on one end and I on the other. Olympia was leading some conversation, mainly entertaining herself and the princess as I kept an ear tuned to the woods.

"I will gather more wood for the fire," Sir Coulee nodded toward the flame that was burning bright as he placed the last collected piece of wood onto it. He stood and stretched before picking up his sword that he had placed propped up against the log.

"I shall go with you." I blinked at the voice and whipped my head toward the Princess. She was beaming toward the knight with brown hair. I opened my mouth but before I could speak, she raised her hand toward me and giggled. "I am sure I can figure out how to collect firewood, Sir Washeen." She elevated her crystal eyes slightly toward me and it was a look I recognized. I forced myself to relax back onto the log and then nodded at her.

Sir Coulee sent a quick look my way, but when the Princess turned toward him, he offered his hand toward the lady. She took it and stood gracefully. She brushed off the back of her dress before walking before the man, leading the way into the woods. He followed her. They disappeared quickly behind luscious green branches. I could hear Sir Coulee saying something and then the wind carried the laughter of the Princess back toward the campsite.

"Why are you always so on guard?" A voice interrupted my focus and I blinked toward the blond haired girl before me. She was stirring the food and it was starting to bubble. The smell drifted toward me and my stomach couldn't help but grumble. "Every time Seattel moves, you are watching her."

"It is my job," I stated, turning my head back toward the woods. I could not hear the two tromping around anymore, yet

I knew that Sir Coulee was a respected gentleman and would not do anything inappropriate. Would he?

Olympia chuckled slightly. "Is it your job to be a stalker?" My eyes snapped back toward the girl. She laughed again, obviously noticing that she got my attention once more. She tasted the stew and then shrugged her shoulders. "I am just saying you could try to give her some area to breathe."

I narrowed my eyes at the girl. "We do not have the luxury to wander right now."

Olympia waved her arms around toward the forest. "She seems safe to me. We have escaped those Gem men and she is with Sir Coulee if anything does happen." There were a few twigs by the fire and she threw the wood into the flame. "Is Sir Coulee not a potential suitor for her?" I did not reply, just simply nodded my head and the lady poked the fire with a little stick. "He seems to be king material. Noble, prideful, a little stuck up," she thought aloud. "Good looking and respectful." I clenched my teeth. Olympia met my eyes once again. "Was he not the one who led part of the army against the Gem's attack from the east? We had a tradesman mention something as he passed through our village a few days back."

"He is. However, I do not care about her suitors. I only care about her safety. Is the stew ready?" I changed the topic. Olympia narrowed her eyes but did not continue the conversation. Instead she handed me a piece of bark that was washed clean in the river and scooped some mouthwatering food onto it.

"If you would have given me more time, I could have packed some bowls."

"Bowls or death, that was your choice."

The girl huffed but did not argue. She scooped herself some food and sat opposite of myself on the log. She took a few bites and smacked her lips at the hot stew. "Do you think Kenne will try to come find me?"

"I do not know." I listened to the woods once again, trying hard to hear any conversation or laughter that could be coming from the knight or Princess. However, all I heard was the chirping birds and a light breeze drifting through the trees.

I also did not want to have this conversation with the farmer girl. I would not be the bearer of bad news.

"When I first met Kenne, my father was a little suspicious of him." She giggled at a memory that I would never be able to see. "He thought he was too well dressed for his age. When Kenne told my father that he was Village Leader, my father could not believe his ears." Olympia scraped some dirt with her shoe and continued talking. I tried to listen to the woods once again but her voice was interrupting me. "My father talked with me and told me that the decision was up to me, but that Kenne was the man to give me the best life." She looked up at me and I half acknowledged her conversation by nodding my head. She ate more stew and I hoped that was the end of the talk.

The girl kept chatting. "Kenne was from Thornwood, but I was from Woodinville. He traveled a few days to reach my village." She was beaming and her familiar smile stretched over her face. I glanced down at my empty piece of bark and stood to get more. "He was searching for a wife and said that my smile stood out in the fields." With my back facing Olympia, I scooped more stew.

It was a typical romance story. "And now he is my beloved," she sighed happily. I returned to my log and took my seat once again. "I sure hope he is okay," she frowned once again.

"I am sure he is fine."

"Did you not find him before you saw the Gems?"

I stood from my seat quickly and turned to the woods, refusing to take part in this conversation any longer. "It should not take this long to collect firewood." I placed my bark down on the log but before I could head into the forest, Princess Seattel emerged from the greenery. Sir Coulee was following close behind. Princess Seattel was smiling. Sir Coulee was smirking. She held five or so pieces while the knight behind her flexed his pile of at least fifteen. With a swift arm movement, both had placed the wood beside the fire.

"The stew is ready?" Princess Seattel smiled at Olympia as the girl jumped up to serve the Princess.

"Find enough wood?" I asked the knight as he dusted the few grass strands that lingered on his clothes. I winced at how sarcastic my question had been as we are surrounded by forest.

The knight did not seem to notice and grabbed a piece of bark. "Should be enough to last through the night. I can do first watch."

I nodded and watched as the Princess scooped a serving of stew on a bark piece. She forced a smile and thanked Olympia for the delicious food. Was she grateful for the food? Yes. The plates? No. She had only eaten on fine china all her life and even the clay plates at the farmer's girl's house were 'dirty' enough for her. She glanced at my bark and I demonstrated to her, scooping some food with my fingers before eating the yummy chunks. Looking at her own fingers, she frowned. But, since there were no fancy knives, or the pronged version she used, which I believe were called forks, she sat on the log and accepted her fate.

I refused to show any emotion on my face, although I had a hard time not laughing as Princess Seattel delicately ate a chunk of stew. I relaxed back into my regular position, with my hand on the hilt of my sword. I did not like the Princess out of my sight. Especially with Coulee.

Chapter 13

After dinner, Olympia collected our bark pieces and burned them in the flames. Princess Seattel did not eat any of the stew that directly touched the wood and she watched it disintegrate in the fire before her.

We had an evening of talks, mainly the two ladies, as they shared childhood stories. It was interesting to hear the differences between the two and it was amazing that they got along. Princess Seattel had talked about using the servant corridors and getting caught by her father, King Yakima, while Olympia told tales of stealing her neighbors chicken eggs and hiding them in her front door plants so while she was weeding, she would randomly find an egg.

Sir Coulee chuckled a few times and even shared his input, only stating that he grew up in a family of four older sisters. The two girls then talked about how they wish they had siblings. The Princess' mother had died when she was young and

Olympia was the only child, her parents never able to have more children.

"How many siblings did you have, Washeen?" Olympia asked me. Princess Seattel let out a giggle and then composed herself, sitting straighter on the log when Sir Coulee grinned over at her.

"You would never believe it if he told you."

"You know?" Olympia had glanced at Princess Seattel who had smiled at me.

"Of course," the Princess had told the farmer girl. "Sir Washeen has been my guard for four years now. We know a lot about each other." I ran a hand through my hair and then poked the fire with a stick. "He has taken a few family days here and there." I tried not to make it a habit.

Olympia beamed at me and threw me a couple of berries she had picked from a nearby bush. "Wait! I want to guess!" She scrunched her nose as she thought and then blurted out, "SIX!"

As I shook my head, Princess Seattel laughed and fixed her dress. She turned to look at me with humor in her eyes and I gave her a slight smirk back. "That was not close."

Sir Coulee jumped in as well and I almost smiled at the knight, proud of his guess, sure that it was right. "Either two or eight."

"That is quite the difference," Princess Seattel answered for me. Olympia bounced in her spot on the log before blurting out another guess. Sir Coulee looked a bit disturbed at the unlady-like behavior but like a true knight, he did not comment.

"Ten!?"

Apparently the Princess could not wait for another guess. "He has fifteen other siblings!" I watched as Sir Coulee phys-ically sat back stunned while Olympia's jaw dropped. I waited for someone to speak but nobody made a comment. "I am not lying," the Princess truthfully said. The group glanced at me and I nodded, confirming Princess Seattel spoke the truth.

"There is no way!" Olympia shrieked, loud enough to dam-age someone's hearing if they sat close by. That was a weapon to be reckoned with. "How do you even remember all their names? How could your parents even think of that many names?"

I shrugged. "It is not that hard. Clarkston is the oldest, fol-lowed by my sisters Elma, Lacey, and Roslyn. Then there are the twins, Milton and Morton. My brother Granger is next, then George, me, Edmond, and Roy. Then there is Liberty, my moth-er did not even know she was pregnant, followed by another set of twins, Kirk and Kent. Vader was the last one... or so we thought. Ruston was a surprise two years ago." I could see his reddish hair and his childish grin in my head. I did not mention my siblings' loved ones or their families. "Four girls and twelve boys."

Sir Coulee had spoken up then and I almost grinned again. "That is like a small army!"

"I wish I had that many siblings," Olympia sighed. "I hope for a big family one day."

-=--=-=--=- Guard of the Evergreen Princess -=--=-=--=-

The campfire was dwindling as a few pieces of wood crackled in agony. I rolled over and pressed my hand to my arm, feeling the fresh wrapping tighten comfortably around the recovering wound. An owl hooted in the distance making the Princess take in a quick breath, but not enough noise to stun her out of her sleep. There was a gentle breeze and if listening carefully enough, I could hear the river gushing down the land.

"What is the point of myself staying awake to keep watch if you refuse to lie down?" Sir Coulee asked me, running his eyes over my resting place. He had entered my line of sight and put his hands on his hilt. "I can keep this camp safe while you rest your eyes." I was in a half sitting position with my back resting against a log. My toes were close to the fire and I had removed my boots to stretch the digits.

I met the knight's gaze. "I am not as tired as I expected."

Sir Coulee scoffed, making me wonder yet again what sort of upbringing he had. "And you expect me to believe that. We have traveled throughout the night. It has been at least a day since you have slept." The knight stretched, reaching his arms high as if to prove a point.

I glared. "Can you please move? You are blocking the fire." I scooted across the log so that the flames once again warmed my toes.

"Fine." His voice was curt. "Do not slow us down tomorrow morning." He tromped back into the bushes surrounding the area and continued walking in a giant circle around the camp. I suspected he did this so that he would not doze off sitting and listening to the forest.

I laid my head back and closed my eyes, placing my hand back on my arm and feeling the comfort once again. Sure, sleep was something I did need, but in Thornwood we were attacked in the evening. I could not shake the feeling that something else was coming. My mind darted back to this evening. A smile once again tried to show up on my lips.

My thoughts were interrupted by Princess Seattel turning over in her sleep. She did not have a blanket, but slept close to the fire with Olympia on the other side of her. I closed my eyes once again and continued to rest, but first listened for Sir Coulee's footsteps. Once satisfied that I heard him stomping around, enough noise to scare away any wild beast, I relaxed against the log once more.

But instead of thinking, I felt myself get dragged into a deep dark hole of my mind and I drifted off to sleep.

"Not tired?" A boot kicked my leg and I forced my eyes open. Sir Coulee stood over me and I scowled as I swiped a line of dirt off my trousers. The night was dark and the fire crackled more strongly. Sir Coulee must have added another log to feed the flames.

I stood, readjusting my dark blue waistcoat. With the flickering light I could see the Princess still sound asleep, lulled by
the popping sounds coming from the open flame. Sir Coulee
settled down where I was recently laid and I glanced over to
Olympia who was sitting up on the log with her shawl snugged
around her. A light breeze caused her hair to flutter and she
shivered, pulling her shawl closer against her body. Olympia
met my eyes and gave me a small smile.

I turned and walked out of the camp, starting on the left and
began to circle the group. The forest was quieter at night with
only an owl hoot here and there. No birds were chirping but
the small breeze that fluttered through made the woods seem
safe.

After the inspection I returned to the camp and stood against
a tree. Olympia cleared her throat and moved closer to my
location. I tilted my head at her but did not say anything. The
girl situated herself and then began to talk in a low whisper,
careful not to wake the Princess or the snoring Sir Coulee, who
must have fallen asleep once his head hit the ground.

"It is a beautiful night."

"Why are you not asleep?"

The girl blinked at me before turning back toward the fire. "I
am worried about Kenne."

There were no more words as we both watched the flames
crackle. I ran a hand through my hair and kept my ear tuned

toward the woods. Princess Seattel rolled over in her sleep, twigs and leaves stuck in her long, wavy hair.

The sun would rise in an hour or so, I guessed, from the way the sky looked. The stars were dimming and more clouds were taking over the darkness. I am sure it will rain soon.

"Do you know where we are going from here?" Olympia asked me.

I shook my head. "Not really. I have never been this far away from the castle. Sir Coulee mentioned a town called Lone Pine which offers a boat across the river. We will need to back track but it is a necessity."

"You are taking her south to her troops?"

I nodded. "Yes."

"How old is she?"

I glanced at the girl before shifting my feet into more comfortable and flat ground. The question did startle me. "She is in her twentieth year." Both of us looked over to the Princess. Beside her was the backpack with a few potatoes falling out of it.

Olympia sighed. "She was telling me about Helen." A wave of sadness washed through me but I held my ground and did not show any sign of weakness. "From the way she talked she was close to the girl."

"They were good companions."

"Good friends," Olympia corrected me. "Just because she is a Princess does not mean she cannot have maidservant friends. I consider myself her friend." I slowly nodded my head, agreeing with what the girl was saying. "You and Helen were close as well?"

I silently swallowed. "We had to be. We served the princess." I leaned forward and picked up one of the remaining logs on the ground. Carefully, I set it on the burning pile, not wanting any ashes to leap out.

"You and her were just friends?"

"We worked together."

"Why are you like this?" I blinked at Olympia as her voice became harsh and a tone I never thought would come out of her throat hissed toward me. Sir Coulee stirred, opening his eyes and glaring at us before rolling onto his back and heaving a giant sigh. Olympia continued in a quieter whisper. "You are so strict and stuck up."

The words hit me as a whip and I frowned to myself, making sure I heard her right. She said I was the stuck up one? My eyes darted to Sir Coulee.

"Why can you not admit you were close with Helen? For four years she was a maidservant to Seattel and as you said earlier tonight that you have been Seattel's personal guard for four years as well."

I did not speak. Olympia watched me carefully as I kept a stone face.

There was a scuffing sound to the left that caught our attention. "Can you speak more quietly or better yet; not at all?" Sir

Coulee groaned, rolling to his side once again. "I am exhaust-ed." The knight folded his arm under his head as a makeshift pillow and closed his eyes once again.

Olympia stood, gathering her surcoat in her arms. Before she walked back to her own sleeping spot she turned and spoke. "I am just saying, you need to be more comforting to Seattel. She lost her home and her best friend in one night and was thrown into a different world than what she is used to. She can hide her pain fairly well but I know she is suffering. You protect her physically from harm, but who is protecting her from what is going on on the inside? Her thoughts, feelings, and her heart?" The girl stepped around the fire and I turned my eyes toward the sleeping Princess once again. Her face did seem tense and the sleep was not as peaceful as it usually is. Why had I not noticed this sooner?

No. My job was her personal bodyguard. That is it.

A streak of bright purple and red now ran across the sky as the beginnings of morning began to show. Sir Coulee let me sleep a lot longer than he should have and I felt slightly embarrassed. I pulled at the wrap around my arm, knowing it would need to be cleaned in the river before we continued our route toward Lone Pine.

The Princess tossed in her sleep and I narrowed my eyes at the sight. Sir Coulee also peeked out once again before snap-ping his eyes shut once more. I glared at the knight. He needed to remember that his job was to get her safe and sound to the troops in the south. He did not need to worry about her emotional side.

I could do that.

Olympia had settled down once again. My thoughts ran wild with what she had said. Should I talk to her about what happened with Helen? I comforted her at Thornwood. Did that not help?

Chapter 14

"May we stop?" Princess Seattel took a second to catch her breath before continuing. Her cheeks were a rosy red and she panted in quick gasps. She held her hand to her waist as she fanned herself with her other. Sir Coulee was leading the way up the river, followed by Olympia and Princess Seattel. I took up the rear, eyeing every once in a while behind us, checking that we were not being followed. So far the day was nice, but angry dark clouds seemed to be coming our way. "I need a little moment."

I could tell that Sir Coulee was not the happiest with having to stop and rest, but he nodded toward the Princess and took his own seat on a nearby rock. Olympia grabbed the water canteen and took a few gulps while Princess Seattel tried to wipe some of the sand off a nearby rock, before giving up and sitting on it with her already sandy dress.

A rabbit scurried by and Sir Coulee jumped to his feet. "I will try to catch it now so that we can eat it later." The knight had a good point. I watched as he followed the furry creature closely. Olympia flipped a canteen upside down.

"I will fetch us more water."

Both Princess Seattel and I watched as the girl made her way down the river bed. The water was gushing and the soothing sound was heard from where we were sitting. There were moments of silence before the Princess spoke again.

"Did you sleep well, Washeen?" She fiddled with her hair and cringed as her fingers ran through quite a knotted piece.

"Fairly."

"I miss my bed." I blinked at the lady.

"Likewise."

The Princess heaved a sigh and watched as Sir Coulee located the rabbit's burrow in the clearing before us. "How long do you believe it will be before we make it back to the castle?" She turned to face me.

I adjusted my boots and began to tie a loose lace. "A couple of weeks for sure. We should make it to Lone Pine tonight and from there locate a boat. It will take another three days to reach the south and once we connect with the army and knights, it will be another week or so before they are ready to move south." This was all off of what Sir Coulee had said to me earlier. The knight seemed to know much about the troops and the organization that goes with it.

"My Father already has prepared them." Princess Seattel looked confident in her answer. "Surely he will get there before us?" This was not as much as a question, more of a spoken quote that required me to agree with her.

"Surely." Surely. A nervous feeling echoed through my guts.

"May we stop?" Princess Seattel once again asked. It was about a long moment or so since the last time she had asked. However, it was not long enough for Sir Coulee or myself for that matter, to be happy with the progress we were making. Olympia was chatting the entire trip about everything in this kingdom while Sir Coulee stomped forward, annoyed with the talks that were happening.

Sir Coulee groaned and rolled his head back. "It has only been a short while since our last break." He seemed to remember who he was talking to and added hastily, "my Princess."

The Princess turned away from the knight and huffed, folding her arms over her stomach. Definitely not her typical royal behavior. "I am sorry that I cannot keep up with your pace." This was not true as she had no problem before keeping up. There was something else going on.

"You have done fine before." I raised an eyebrow at the sharp words of Sir Coulee.

The Princess glared at the knight. "Perhaps you forget who you are speaking to." The tone was icy. Her chin was raised and her crystal eyes flashed power at the man before her. He met her gaze and lowered his eyes, slightly bowing.

"As you wish, Princess."

Olympia sat nervously on a log nearby as Sir Coulee began scouting the area around us, making sure it was safe enough to stop. Princess Seattel played with her hands and continued to slowly pace around the area. My eyes narrowed.

"Princess, if you may follow me," I held out my hand for her to grasp. She looked at me questioningly.

"I said I would like a break."

I sent a soft smile for half a second before returning to my stoic look. "This will only take a small moment." She sighed before glancing at Olympia and Sir Coulee who both were trying to watch her unsuspiciously. The Princess then gently took my hand.

I led her into the woods, shooting Sir Coulee a glare when he began to follow. The man smartly reconsidered his idea and sat down on the log next to Olympia. He did not look impressed as she began to talk.

The Princess followed me for a short way before I stopped in front of an enormous mountain. It seemed to be higher than the clouds, with snow covering the tips of it. From our viewpoint you could see thousands of feet around it. The sky stretched for a while before fading out into gray, stormy clouds. I breathed in the fresh air.

"Why are we here?" Princess Seattel asked me as we both admired the enormity of the rock in front of us. She fixed part of her hair before straightening her dress, trying to maintain her social status look. Her chin was raised as she looked up the mountain before her, her posture perfect and precise. She did not look the part, however, with her stained dress and her tangled, matted hair. Her face had a streak of dirt on it and there was more than one twig stuck in her dress.

I did not answer her question right away. Instead, I turned my ear to listen to the woods behind us. The birds were chirping and the wind blew through the trees as usual. It was colder than before, gray clouds starting to loom above us. I could not hear anything suspicious in the woods and so I began to talk. "We are here to remember Helen."

"Oh." Her voice was soft and did not waver, but I could tell I struck a nerve. There was another moment of silence before I picked up a stone and placed it on the grass in front of us. I grabbed another and yet another, making a mock grave for our dear friend. Princess Seattel watched as she tried to hold back the tears. I inwardly thanked Olympia for telling me to put this memory to rest.

Soon, the grave was done. I placed myself onto the rock that Princess Seattel was seated on. Her hands were trembling in her lap and I gently placed my own hand on hers. "We could call this Mount Helen," I suggested to her. Her eyes never wavered from the beautiful sight in front of us.

"I would like that. Mount Helen," she tested the name. The wild flowers that were crawling up the sides of the mountains were blooming now, with pink, red, orange, and yellow colors creating an amazing look. It was so peaceful, with birds chirping and the wind blowing gently at our hair. Princess Seattel sat strong.

I frowned as the clouds grew darker, however, and knew that we needed to head back to the group. "Would you like to say a few final words to Helen?"

The Princess nodded and stood from the rock, fixing her green dress before kneeling beside the grave. At first she began whispering a few things and moving one of the stones I had placed. After a few sentences, she looked at me, her eyes watery. "I miss her, Washeen."

I swallowed hard. I stood and repositioned myself next to the heiress. "I do as well."

Princess Seattel turned back to the rock and continued talking. "I will never forget the first day you were appointed my maid. I thought my father was mad, giving me an inexperienced worker. The first day you brought me burnt bread!" She caught a tear before it fell with her finger and forced herself not to shed another one. "As I complained, you opened my window and chucked it outside, aiming for the pig pen, but it landed in a vendor's vegetables and he could not figure out where it came from!" I felt a smile grow on my face at the reminder of the hilarious scene.

"You quickly became my friend. I hated it when you called me by a title like 'princess'. I did not feel the need for you to do so, although it was particularly funny when you and Sir Washeen continued to tease me with them." She gave me a weak smile. "Not funny at the time, but it is funny now."

I smirked a bit and then glanced at the mountain once again. Princess Seattel continued to talk. "The first week you woke me up late and I missed my morning breakfast with my father. I remember him knocking on my chambers and you were so fearful that I faked I was not feeling well." A little giggle escaped her mouth before she continued talking. "After that, I faked being sick more than once so that we could spend most of the day together. I still do not know why you continued to challenge me at chess; you have never won a game." The memories were also fond in my head as I can recall the laughter that would echo through the chamber doors. More than once I would have to remind the ladies that Princess Seattel was supposed to be sick.

The topic that the Princess was talking about changed again. "I really wish you were here, Helen." I watched as Princess Seattel moved another rock. "We are heading south toward my father and the troops and we are traveling with Sir Coulee and a girl called Olympia." She paused and added a side note. "You would get along great with her." Her eyes wandered to the mountain. "I am going to miss all the memories that could have been, but I am going to treasure the ones that we have had." A few raindrops began to fall and I frowned.

"We need to head soon," I reminded the Evergreen Princess. She nodded and used a hand to push back the long black hair that fell over her shoulder onto some of the rocks.

"I will always love you, Helen. You were the best friend I could ever ask for."

Princess Seattel began to stand and I quickly offered my hand, which she used. Before I could let go, however, she pulled me into a hug. "Thank you, Washeen."

I moved the Princess away from me, shocked at the physical touch. "Princess!"

She pulled me closer. "Nobody is watching. Besides, can friends not hug?" At this I pondered. I knew that yes, they could hug. But also, hugging a girl who was not your beloved was inappropriate, was it not? And hugging a Princess was even more inappropriate, I am sure! Before I could even voice my opinion, Princess Seattel hugged me again. There was a slight tremor that went through her body and this time, I did not stop her. As soon as my arms wrapped around the small of her back, the tears started to fall and I held the sobbing girl tight.

Something moved in my heart.

The rain began to pour.

Chapter 15

Sir Coulee shook his head, hair flying everywhere and the droplets of water following suit. It did not make a difference, however, as the downpour only seemed to drench his roots once again. He ran a hand through his hair, forcing it out of his face, before motioning toward some wood that was hidden under tree roots and moss. "That should be dry enough."

I nodded and took as many sticks as I could carry, using my body as a shield from the rain before heading over toward the temporary shelter. The girls were trying to use the flickering flame to cook the rabbit that Sir Coulee had caught before. We had tied the blanket up in the tree to make a run off for the buckets of water that were raining from the sky.

"Here." I placed the sticks on top of the small fire and sighed in relief as I watched the flame start to lick. The last thing we needed was the Princess to get sick on our journey to the south. Princess Seattel handed me the canteen.

"We are almost out of water." Olympia frowned and shook Sir Coulee's canteen, making the little bit of water left inside, slosh around. "Perhaps you could set up some sort of collector?" She glanced toward me.

I nodded. "It should be possible." I began to dig in the soil, creating a spot where the canteen would be able to sit and catch water.

Princess Seattel sat with her back against the trunk. "If only we knew how close we were to Lone Pine and if it is worth it for us to walk through this horrible, dreaded weather." A clash of thunder echoed through the woods, almost perfect timing to Sir Coulee clumsily tramping through the bushes. He had a few more logs to add to the fire. A flash of lightning lit up the area for mere moments before vanishing.

"We are not walking through this," Sir Coulee informed the Princess. I had noticed that the knight was beginning to relax on the formalities with the Princess, not something that I was very happy about. He was a knight and he should know that he must continue to treat her with the utmost respect. He took an oath, after all.

"But what if Lone Pine is right around the corner?"

I spoke up, agreeing with the knight. "It would be better to stay as dry as possible. We do not want you-any of us to get sick." I felt a red flush go to my face and I tilted my head down, fixing the canteen into the perfect position.

Sir Coulee placed the logs beside Princess Seattel to keep them dry. "Is the rabbit almost ready?" He directed the question to Olympia.

"It is if you consider a raw food diet," Olympia spoke toward the man, not turning to face him. Sir Coulee looked taken aback and I held back a smirk at the scene. She rotated the rabbit over the flames and sat back on her haunches, ripping up some sort of green spice she found in the woods and sprinkling it on top of the meat. Sir Coulee looked over her shoulder.

"How do you know if that is safe to eat?" he asked, an eyebrow raised as she rubbed the green plant overtop of the rabbit.

Olympia shrugged. "I fed some to you the first night you stayed with us and you are still with us." She glanced at the knight with a sparkle in her eye. "You did not get sick from it, did you?"

"I did not!"

Princess Seattel covered a smile with her hand to be polite but a small giggle was heard. Our eyes met and I ended up smirking at the knight's expense as well.

I watched as the Princess pushed a few stray pieces of hair out of her face and behind her ears. How she managed to still look royal in her wet, borrowed dress, I do not know. Her hair was a giant knot that Olympia had twisted behind her head and tied with a strip of cloth from the bottom of her dress. The farmer girl had talked about how cutting it shorter would be easier but the Princess strongly refused. I did not think she had ever had short hair.

I set up the last canteen and sighed, placing myself under the blanket above us. The rain soaked everything in the woods and the thunder was not letting up. It would probably be a sleepless night for us.

"No potatoes?" Sir Coulee gruffly wondered, settling himself on an overturned tree. He was still bitter about lugging the roots through the woods before.

Olympia took a sigh before turning to the knight. "I thought you could use a break from eating that root." She poked at the fire. "In reality, I did not believe that the fire would be warm enough to cook it." She made a face. "I do not like raw potatoes."

Sir Coulee opened his mouth but then decided against it as Olympia tossed a potato in the air and caught it with ease. She grinned at him, knowing he wanted to speak but had decided not too.

After all, I would not like a raw potato thrown at me either. Olympia already displayed her upbringing and I believe she would have no problem in 'disrespecting' the knight by chucking the food.

The fire crackled. The rabbit began to smell amazing and Olympia flipped it a few more times. Then, satisfied, she picked up the meat and poked it towards Sir Coulee. "Thank you for your patience, Coulee. You may have the first piece." She placed the rabbit on a strip of bark and motioned toward me. I pulled the dagger from my boot and the farmer girl began to cut the meal.

Sir Coulee cleared his throat. "I insist the Princess eat first," he told the girl. Although it was a knightly, selfless action, I narrowed my eyes at the man. Some rain dripped onto his boot.

Princess Seattel, however, was flattered. "How gracious, Sir Coulee." She gave the man a slight nod and accepted her food from Olympia. She smiled through clenched teeth, seeing her meal was once again, on a strip of bark. We made eye contact for a second, before she turned and smiled again at the knight beside her, taking a delicate bite out of the rabbit. Sir Coulee gently moved one of her strands of hair that was entwined in the tree's bark behind her, to her shoulder. Another royal smile was directed at the man.

Everyone had a few strips of meat and Sir Coulee placed a log on the fire. Olympia picked up one of the canteens and took a sip. A crack of a twig caught my attention and I instantly turned, listening for any noise coming in the same direction. For a moment everything seemed calm, peaceful almost. I watched the breeze directed raindrops to the left.

Thunder roared again and I squinted past the downpour of rain. A flash of red startled me and a whistling sound drowned out the rain's common noise.

"Get down!"

An arrow pegged the canteen out of Olympia's hand and stuck it straight to a tree. The girls gasped at the water flooding out of the hole before Sir Coulee and myself launched ourselves on top of them. A shout was heard before two more arrows lodged themselves in the tree.

"Don't kill the girl! Take her alive." The roar was almost demon-like.

"Run!" Sir Coulee bellowed. It was unnecessary.

I already fled the scene with the Princess over my shoulder, a shriek leaving her throat. The sound of metal clanging with metal filled the woods and I darted a look back. A flash of lightning lit up the scene. Sir Coulee battled with two Gem warriors. He barely dodged the axe coming toward his head. My feet pounded on the forest floor.

I leapt over a few fallen trees before darting through the closest bushes. Ahead was a small dirt incline and water was creating small falls down the dirt. My heart sank. There was no way I would be able to climb that with Princess Seattel over my shoulder. I set her down but before she could even catch her breath, I pulled her with me and began the incline. I had an iron grasp on her wrist.

I glanced back to see Olympia following, her face pale. Thunder drowned out all sound in the woods for a moment before Sir Coulee burst through the bushes. There was a small cut above his eye.

"Four more to the left!" he yelled, his sword at the ready. He stood at the base of the hill and gutted a stray Gem who followed him through the brush. I let go of Princess Seattel's hand and climbed a bit ahead before turning, grabbing her hand again and practically launching her up the hill. Her hair tie caught on my belt and her black hair fell loose but the Princess seemed not to notice as I forced her forward.

"Olympia!" The Princess tried to reach her hand down to the farmer girl but I pushed her farther up.

"Go!"

She had no choice but to continue. Sir Coulee yelled out something behind us, but the thunder drowned him out. The mud was slick.

I managed to get the Princess up the slope before myself. I turned for a moment, just being able to catch Sir Coulee striking another Gem. The rain was so heavy I couldn't see whether or not the hit had been fatal. Olympia was about half way up the dirt incline.

I put my arm around the Princess' waist, ignoring the slimy dirt handprint it left on her dress. We ran farther away from the men, dodging in and out of trees. The rain pounded down and all the branches were hanging low. It was hard to see or hear anything besides the rain.

The Princess let out a few breathless gasps but did not slow. We ran for a few minutes, yanking her dress through a particularly thorny bush. It was rather stuck and the Princess and

I frantically yanked at the material. I did not care if the dress ripped. I needed to get her to safety. With a final, hard tug, the dress came loose. I grabbed her hand but before even taking a few more steps, a startled, pained cry came from the Princess.

"Sir Washeen." She fell to her knees and desperately tugged at her black locks that were deeply tangled in the brush. It must have matted as we pulled on her dress.

I did a test pull and she whimpered. The hair was twisted and woven deep into the bush, almost as if she had somersaulted through. I reached for my dagger and pulled it from my boot. My hand felt heavy and I swallowed hard. Her eyes met mine. "No," she whispered.

But I knew. There was no way I would be able to untangle this in time. I did a quick glance around the area before kneeling beside her. She grasped a few strands and tried to pull once more. Tears sprang into her eyes.

"It will take a moment." I gently moved her head as far away from the bush as I could. A few branches clung desperately to the locks. She gripped my hand with her own and I refused to meet her eyes.

"Please. No."

It was a quick slice. I swallowed hard at the sight of her hair left in the bush and forced myself to her feet. She bowed her head and stayed seated in the mud. I shoved the feelings down and hardened my look. I sheathed the dagger.

Silence followed. I placed my arm around her waist and helped her to her feet. We began to move forward again. She did not look back. Her dress was heavy with rain and mud and I debated if I should hide her and wait this out, or if it would be beneficial to gain more distance. I swallowed hard, looking at her red rimmed eyes and knowing that the rain falling was washing away any signs of tears.

There was a shout behind us and I used my body to knock the Princess to the left, behind a fallen tree. She crawled under the brush as quickly as she could and I knelt nearby, my sword drawn and ready. A flash of lightning lit up the area and the Gem with the red surcoat entered my vision. I was unsure whether it was thunder roaring through my ears or the man in front of me.

"Washeen." My focus moved for a split second, resulting in a quick swallow. The tears were heavy in her eyes and her chin trembled for a second. An oddly cut strand of hair fell into her eyes. The rest settled just below her ears.

Another flash of lightning. My hand gripped the hilt of the sword. A familiar spot. It took only a few moments for him to be at arm's length.

Chapter 16

In a split second, my eyes met his; pools of inky rage and fury stared out of his soulless face. His cheekbones were raised and hard, his entire face heavily tattooed to resemble some kind of wolf. He stood about a head taller than me, and his red surcoat, made of dyed animal furs, was torn open, exposing his bare chest. It was covered in vicious scars. His muscular arms tensed and rippled as his right hand gripped a vicious looking morningstar, the spiky ball encrusted in gore. Its chain was rusty and coated in mud.

The Gem opened his mouth wide and let out a furious roar that sounded like a thunderclap in my ears.

His morningstar swung in a wild arc at my head and I desperately swung my sword to block the swing. The chain looped around past my sword with an ominous clanking sound, the spiky ball grazing my cheek. I felt the sting of blood.

The Gem slammed his knee upward and into my gut, forcing me backward as I struggled to keep my footing on the muddy forest floor. In response, I wrenched my sword downward, out of the metallic grip of the morningstar's chain, and thrust my other hand forward. It slammed into the Gem's exposed chest. It felt like punching a wall and he hardly flinched. His left hand lunged forward, grabbing my sword arm and immobilizing it with pain. I felt my bones creaking under the pressure. I slammed my free hand's fist against his face over and over again as he crushed my arm. I felt his cheekbones cracking and his teeth breaking and he roared out in wrath, but he did not relent. I knew he would break my arm soon.

Using all my weight, I threw myself backward onto the mud of the forest floor, feeling small shrubs and twigs break under me. The Gem was caught off guard by this and his weight threw him off balance. He collapsed onto the forest floor beside me with a thud. Our weapons were of no use here and we both knew it. Rapidly reaching out with my right hand, I caught a fistful of his thick disheveled hair, yanking his head back as his hands grasped wildly about. I bashed his head into the forest floor, his face smashing against an exposed root of a nearby tree. I heard the shattering of facial bone and saw the wolf tattooed face deform and warp as I forced it downward again and again. He roared and began twisting to get loose.

I desperately grasped for anything to use as a weapon and I felt a dead branch, still grafted in the trunk of the tree. I wrenched against the dead branch with all my might, snapping it free as the rain gushed down through my eyes. The branch was about the length of a shortsword. Rush after rush of pain ripped through my arm as the Gem grabbed a hold of it once again. Gripping the branch as well as I could, I stabbed it down and into the Gem warrior's gut and embedded it into the Gem's abdomen. He roared in pain and released my arm.

There was too much rain to see clearly. With a grunt, I wrenched the branch free, and holding it in both hands I rammed it upward against his throat. With each hit, I felt his trachea crunching and crumbling as the Gem warrior's thick hands grasped wildly about the forest floor.

Finally, with a soft thud, his hands fell limp on the muddy ground, the rain washing away the blood and bits of bone from his broken facial structure. His mouth slumped open. Not hearing any other human sounds, I fumbled about on the forest floor until I felt the cold hilt of my sword, which I grasped tightly and brought to my side, using it as a support to help myself stand. I took a step, and felt my foot make contact with something else, unnatural, metallic. It was the Gem's morningstar.

I blinked furiously, trying to get the water out of my eyes to locate the Princess. She peered out from behind the fallen tree. "Sir Washeen?" Her voice was hesitant as she quickly glanced at the fallen warrior. "Are you alright?" Her usually picture perfect hair was cut lopsided and her cheeks were smeared with mud.

I glanced around the area before shaking my head, water droplets flying everywhere. My sword was sheathed with a practiced movement. "No need to worry about me, my

Princess." I left the body behind and moved closer to the Princess. Princess Seattel narrowed her eyes but seemed to accept the statement. I willed my breath to ease. My body ached here and there but that was to be expected.

There was movement in the bush before Olympia staggered out, completely covered in mud. If not for the familiar blond hair, there would be no recognizing the girl. I held back a smirk. Olympia ran up to the Princess and hugged her tight. "I am so happy you are alright!" she breathed, pieces of mud falling off her arms in the process. "I was worried!" My eyes darted around for any other danger.

The Princess smiled weakly, placing her arms around the other girl daintily, my guess would be to avoid the mud as much as possible. "I am pleased to see that you are fine as well!" The rain continued to pour and I herded the girls under a nearby tree.

"We must still be quiet," I informed them. "There still could be Gems around." My sentence was barely finished before a clap of thunder boomed through the trees. Another clang came from behind the bushes before a flash of silver caught my eyes.

"Get down!" I hissed to the girls and they dropped like rocks. The mud covered farmer girl blended in quite well with the ground and Princess Seattel clung close to the roots of the tree. I darted behind a nearby tree and kept an eye on the silver movement in the bush. The rain poured down hard, making the movement harder to see.

Sir Coulee tumbled from the brush and landed heavily on his side. In a few quick moments, he was back on his feet and charging back into the greenery. Before he made it that far, another brute appeared. The girls were out of sight behind the tree and continued to go unnoticed by the man. He began to circle the knight, a sword in each hand and his golden teeth gleaming. "Trapped you now, Sir Knight," he mocked. "My fellow Gem is only a moment away." He opened his mouth and howled. "KOOT!"

Sir Coulee fixed his stance, sword at the ready. He swung but it was blocked by the brute, who retaliated with a hit of his own. Sir Coulee knocked it to the side.

"I will give you some advice," Sir Coulee's voice echoed bravely. He shook his head, trying to get the wet hair out of his face. "Leave now, before it is too late." He almost had to yell to be heard over the downpour of the rain and the occasional thunder boom. The knight ran a hand through his hair, slicking it back. "I have already killed four of you."

"But you cannot defeat me!" the gruff voice practically bellowed and the Gem warrior began to laugh towards the knight. "I am at least twice as strong and once my fellow soldier shows up, you will have no hope." He then turned and bellowed into the bushes once more. "KOOTENAI!"

There was a reply to that shout, although distant. I could not hear the words as the rain roared. Olympia motioned to me, most likely wondering why I had not joined Sir Coulee's side of the battle. I ignored the signals.

Simple. Sir Coulee was not the Princess. And a trained knight, like the one before us, should be able to defeat this Gem warrior. I had no doubt as I watched the man. If the Gem warrior spotted me, there is no doubt that he would know the Princess was close by. My clothing, like Sir Coulee's, sported the king's emblem. I focused on Sir Coulee once more, the cut above his brow had seemed to stop bleeding and his left arm had mud smears. Otherwise, the man was in excellent shape for taking down four brutes.

The man took a menacing step forward, water running down his bald head. Sir Coulee got his sword at the ready once again. "I will give you some advice," the Gem ridiculed again. "All we need is the Princess. Give us the girl, and you can walk free." Lightning flashed.

Sir Coulee snorted in disbelief. "You would not miss the chance to gut me like a pig."

The man froze and smiled, an eerily, toothy grin. "Not as dumb as you look." And with that, he swung. Sir Coulee evenly matched the blows and managed to throw in a kick here and there. The Gem's fighting was gruesome and spine-chilling, while Sir Coulee used training and expertise. It was mere moments before Sir Coulee had forced the man to unhand his weapons. There was no hesitation as his sword went straight through the vermin's gut, the knight putting all his weight on his end of the blade, ensuring death.

Once he stood again, Sir Coulee took a deep breath and threw back his hair. The rain seemed to let up a bit, although the thunder still rolled overhead. Darkness was covering the woods fast. Before the girls could struggle to their feet, a body flew out of the bush once again. This time, it was another Gem, younger than the one prior, and before I could shout a warning, he had collided with Sir Coulee, axe in hand. The two struggled in the mud, slipping as each tried to get the upper hand. It took only one more hit before the Gem, my guess Kootenai, was in the better position, standing and axe raised. I ran from my spot, unsheathing my sword. But before I could make it, expecting to plunge my sword in from behind, a girl with golden hair stabbed her dagger into the shoulder of the man.

Startled, the man fell forward and Olympia, with the blade still embedded and her grip on the dagger, fell with him. The dirt a few feet away was just as muddy as the spot Sir Coulee laid on. However, the ground beneath them disappeared, sucking the two bodies with it. One moment they were there, the next they were not.

"Olympia!" The scream was desperate. Princess Seattel skittered out from her spot by the tree as I peered over the cliff that had presented itself. The rushing river was below. There was no sight of either the Gem or the farmer girl. Sir Coulee stood next to me on the ledge. I ran a hand through my hair and began looking over the area that Olympia had fallen into, ignoring the panic feeling filling my entire being. The Princess clutched my arm and cried silently, trembling like a leaf, and I placed my arm around her frame, holding her up.

"There!" he pointed out. I followed his finger and saw a bit of blond hair submerging beneath the crashing water. Sir Coulee's gaze glanced at the Princess and took in her pale appearance. I held my ground. Without another moment, the knight leapt off the ledge, plunging into the dark blue water. Another bellowing sound of thunder echoed in the area.

Princess Seattel let out a hoarse scream and clutched my arm. I tensed. "We have to follow the river!" she cried, beginning to drag me down a nearby slope. I let her lead. One hand clasped the Princess', the other gripping the familiar handle of my sword.

Chapter 17

Darkness fell throughout the woods as a thick blanket. Princess Seattel frantically looked out at the river, finally reaching its rushing side. The rain had calmed, although thunder was still booming overhead. If she felt cold, she showed no signs. "There!" Her voice pierced through my thoughts and I followed her finger until it landed on an amazing sight.

Sir Coulee, coughing, was struggling to his feet by a nearby shore, dragging Olympia's drenched form. He pulled on her dress, now clean of all the mud. The heiress next to me let out a sob and ran down the shore, tripping and slipping over the rocks in her hurry to reach her friend's side. I followed, arms ready to catch the Princess if she fell.

The knight had collapsed next to the farm girl, spitting out liquid and gasping for breath. His clothes stuck tightly to his body as he shivered from the cold, icy water. His breaths came out in the form of a white cloud and as I looked closer, I could not see one coming from the girl next to him.

"Olympia!" The Princess landed on her knees next to the maiden and rolled her over so that her head was to the side. Water pooled out from her mouth, but still no breath was taken in. I assisted Princess Seattel and helped her roll the Olypmia completely over.

I had never seen someone drown. I had heard horror stories in the castle about a few kids drowning in a village over and how their lips first turned blue from the cold. I looked at Olympia's, but could not tell as the darkness was now fully upon us. The moon darted between clouds. "We need to get a fire going!" I shouted toward Sir Coulee, who heaved a cough once more before forcing himself up. He headed into the near-by woods. I turned toward the Princess.

"We need to keep her warm." Princess Seattle nodded at me and with as much haste that she could muster, she pulled the ties off her dress and yanked the fabric over her head. We settled the material around the girl and I felt her neck. A heartbeat fluttered underneath my fingertips. Princess Seattel wrapped her arms around herself, trying to contain the sobs. Her white nightgown was completely stained from the adventure we had taken through the woods. I pulled off my surcoat and handed it to my grace. She gratefully wore it over her sleeping clothes, fingers fumbling with the buttons.

Sir Coulee darted back faster than I expected. He placed the wood down and frantically began using flint and steel to hopefully make a spark catch on the dead grass he had gathered.

Luckily, the fire was on our side and it took ahold of not only the grass, but the small twigs as well. We made eye contact. The Princess grasped Olympia's hand.

"Have you had experience with drownings?" I questioned the knight in front of me. Unfortunately, he shook his head. My shoulder dropped and I took a heavy breath. This did not bode well for Olympia. The warmth of the fire crackled and although her lips were not blue, they were quite pale.

"I have heard a story," the knight suddenly stated, "in a village close to the Gem's border. There was a young girl that fell through the ice in the winter. The physician used both hands and pushed on her chest multiple times and it forced the water out of her." I paused for a second, before hearing a sniffle come from the Princess next to me.

"Olympia! Not you too!" Her voice cracked and she shook the girl.

I motioned toward Olympia and the knight pulled off his gloves. He turned the girl onto her back and began using his weight to push down. It seemed strange, but I was willing to try anything.

Strange or not, it worked. It was only a few pushes from Sir Coulee and the farmer girl spit out water. A strangled gasp came from her before I rolled her over to her side again. More water than I believed was possible was ejected. But, there was breath. And then a few tears.

"Thank you Sir Coulee! Thank you."

The fire crackled warmly, casting shadows along the tree line. The thunder and lightning had stopped a few moments back. The two girls were settled as close to the flames as they dared and Sir Coulee and I checked every now and again that they were still breathing. Princess Seattel's dress laid over the two of them as a blanket.

"That was a close one," the knight suddenly spoke, soft so as not to wake the sleeping ladies. He used a stick and poked the flames. His clothes, although still damp, had dried enough so that they were not dripping wet. A stack of relatively dry wood was next to him. He had searched for a while for the logs while I helped the girls settle on the sand beside the fire. I had warmed up some water and they both drank the warm liquid gratefully.

I murmured my agreement, laying my head back on the tree behind me. I could not get the image of Princess Seattel fiercely hugging Sir Coulee in relief out of my head.

"Let us hope we get to Lone Pine soon." Sir Coulee plunged his sword into the dirt nearby, signalizing he was going to call it a night. There was no discussion about the first watch. "I would not mind sleeping in a proper bed again."

I turned my head toward the Princess again. She was still fast asleep. I stood and placed another log gently on the fire, trying not to have sparks fly out. "Which knight is with the troops down south?" I asked the knight before me. "Sir Kelso?" As one of the King's personal favorite knights, he was involved in a lot of the organizing and leading of the troops.

Sir Coulee shook his head. "I believe it is Sir Walla." He stretched his arms out above his head and then out in front of himself, yawning. "I would not worry about the troops. Sir Walla is very capable."

I sighed. "I just want to make sure that once we get south, we can get the Princess back to the castle and the throne as soon as possible." A light breeze went through the treetops, making a few stray drops of water spray down. Trying to lighten the mood, I added in, "And possibly, a haircut."

Sir Coulee looked at me closely before a small grin was worn. "I noticed she was a little uncomfortable about how it looked." The quick cut I did earlier in the woods was more lopsided than I had thought. We both let out a small chuckle before the woods went back into silence with the odd breeze here and there and a crackle from the fire.

Sir Coulee broke the silence. He motioned toward Princess Seattel. "You know her situation better than almost anyone." The knight paused and I thought that maybe he was going to not ask his question. "With her twentieth ball, was there any suitors that she would marry for the gain of her kingdom?"

It was an odd question. I studied the man before me, who found an interest in picking one of the loose threads on his set of gloves. "The only one ever mentioned was Prince Eugene of the Beaverland, but both of them, including the Kings, agreed their friendship was best. It would be too messy to try to merge the kingdoms into one land." The fire crackled.

Sir Coulee nodded. "The King wanted her to find a potential suitor in the kingdom, then."

I met his eyes. "Yes." I narrowed my eyes. "Is there a reason why you are asking me about this, Sir Coulee?"

Sir Coulee sighed and met my gaze once again, face serious this time. "You must know that in this raid, the King did not make it out alive." The shudder of shock that I had expected to go throughout my body did not. I believe, deep down, I had known the entire time. I kept my voice strong.

"I knew there was a possibility."

Sir Coulee huffed, frustrated, I guessed more at the situation than me dodging whether or not I knew the truth. "I had raced toward his chambers when the Gems attacked. However, I could not make it as there were too many enemy men in the way. So many knights were already gone." He hung his head for a moment. Then, he continued to speak. "I was forced to move through another hallway when I saw you and the Princess leave her quarters." The man sighed. "I was delayed by some of the Gem warriors, but when I defeated them, I could not find you or the Princess. I figured you would try to get her out of the castle and it was by chance that I located you in the woods." He placed his hand to his neck, as if the memory of my sword against his throat still caused physical pain. "I knew the only thing that was needed now was to keep her alive." His gaze went back to the sleeping heiress. "You are doing a decent job at that." I inwardly glared at the half compliment that could still be taken as an insult.

There was a moment of silence before the knight spoke again. "The only reason the Gems are this deep into the kingdom, and the only reason the King would not have his knights and troops searching the countryside for the Princess, is because he is dead. But we should not tell the Princess. It would only crush her."

I looked at the knight, unsure if he was saying this because he did not want to tell her, or if he actually believed it would crush her. "I will not lie if I am asked," I finally spoke.

The King was dead. It was a hard thought to swallow. We both sat in silence, watching the flames eat up another log of dry wood. Sir Coulee picked up the stick once again and began poking the fire. "We need to get her to the south."

I looked at the knight. "I know."

He rubbed his head and ran a hand through his dark brown hair, forcing it back and making it look quite like bed hair. I studied the man once again, remembering what the King had told Princess Seattel in the hallway after the ball.

"I give you my blessing with Sir Coulee. A pure noble blood knight named a war hero a month ago is more than worthy to become a king, ruling alongside you."

Was he king material? I did not believe so. A knight, for sure. He had the physique, handsome enough looks, and the behavior of a nobleman, not to mention the pureblood. I could even add enough battle experience to the list as well. But king material? No.

At least, not yet.

Chapter 18

"Is that the town?"

"I believe so," I agreed. In the distance, there were quite a lot of settlements, with smoke coming out of the chimneys and the backs of the houses along the river. Some boats were docked and ready. A few were crossing the river, the noonday sun high in the sky. There was a homey feeling about the place, whether it be the kids laughing and playing tag on the riverbank, the mothers hanging up laundry to dry in the delightful, sunny day, or the fathers chopping wood, fishing on the lake, or building a few newer houses beside the forest.

Olympia gazed at the sight, smiling as a few kids played hide and seek in their mothers laundry lines. "They all seem so happy."

It was true. Almost everyone that was in sight was smiling or laughing. Sir Coulee continued to lead the way, treading down the hill towards the town. The grass still supported drops of twinkling water from last night's storm, but the sun created a beautiful, fresh look to the area.

We walked into the brick streets of the town, through the markets and the traders. Some had baked goods, while others flaunted pricey materials. I watched as Princess Seattel eyed up some smooth, emerald green silk, obviously from afar and very exquisite. I could tell she longed for home.

"Excuse me, good sir." Sir Coulee stopped an older gentleman, carrying an armload of fishing nets. "Could you tell us where we could go to find someone to borrow a boat from?"

The old man nodded and grinned, taking in the knight's clothing. "Sure thing, Sir Knight. Take a left at the next turn and continue to walk until you can no more. There, you will find a worn down shack." He was missing a few teeth. "Seems sketchy, but the best boating business in town!"

"Thank you, good sir."

A tip of the hat was the reply, before the older gentleman turned away. Sir Coulee continued to lead the group, taking a left at where the man had stated. The walk was a lovely one, the rush of the river getting closer and the warmth of the sun, heating our weary bones. Olympia was practically skipping along, running slightly ahead so she could marvel at the traders' supplies. One would not be able to tell of her near drowning experience, other than the harsh cough she emits.

"Ooh! Seattel! Check out these rings!" There was a squeal from the blond haired girl and the group was halted as the Princess followed. I glanced over her shoulder at the fancy, shimmery jewelry.

Sir Coulee impatiently stood, tapping his foot ever so slightly on the red bricks. "Can we continue on? I am sure the south has just as nice trades." Olympia pulled the Princess over to another booth with embroideries.

"I have never been in another town's marketplace!" Princess Seattel goggled at the rows of tissues. "These items are different than the traders' back at the palace." I did not tell her that she had only been to the nobleman's marketplace. She would find a lot more interesting items in Evergreen's own marketplace, had she been allowed to venture deeper in the lower town. "Such odd items!" She fingered a small roped bracelet.

The man at the booth completed his transaction with another customer. He turned and came up to the ladies. "Anything I can help you with, my fair ladies?" He did a slight bow before pulling out another tray of roped bracelets.

"We were just leaving, thank you," Sir Coulee interrupted, giving the man a polite bow before ushering the ladies away from the table. Before they had a chance to take a step, the man held out a piece of fabric to Olympia.

"For your friend." He motioned toward Princess Seattel. Flustered, she ran her hands through her hair. I nodded my thanks. Olympia twisted the Princess' hair into a bun and wrapped the cloth around it, tying it in place. The lopsided cut was hidden.

When we were a few steps away, Sir Coulee spoke again. "Let us find the man who will rent us a boat." Princess Seattel's face fell, but she nodded. Sir Coulee gently continued. "When we get to safety, you may look at markets there."

We headed toward the river. A small, run down shack seemed to sit on the water. There were some old boards leading into the doorway as a bridge over a small gutter full of water in the street. Sir Coulee stepped onto the makeshift bridge first, and once he was across, offered his hands to the ladies. I refused help.

Inside the shack there were small rafts, fishing nets, and an older man, rocking in his chair and smoking a pipe. "Good day!" he cheerfully spoke, standing from his seat. The boards beneath his feet creaked with the effort of supporting his weight. "How may I be of service?" He eyed Sir Coulee's uniform and the seal of Evergreen on my shoulder. "Especially to you, Sir Knights."

I spoke up. "We are looking to borrow a boat to cross the river."

He gave a toothy grin. "You have come to the right place!"

"I bet the fish are as big as my foot! I should reach down and grab one for dinner," Olympia said to Princess Seattel, looking down into the deep, blue water. The boat that we had 'rented' was more of a raft than it was a boat. Rented was also a strong word. As none of us carried any money with us, and Sir Coulee and myself refused to give up our swords, the old man decided to let us go, considering it as a favor. Princess Seattel promised she would send a man back to pay him in full, but I guess the old man did not believe her and therefore sent us across with the most undesirable boat.

"I would believe they are more like the size of Sir Washeen's sword," Princess Seattel said to Olympia. "I doubt you would be able to catch one. Something that size must be heavy."

"How do you know?"

Princess Seattel smiled and gazed into the water alongside the blond girl. Sir Coulee continued to row. "My tutor taught me."

Olympia looked amazed. "You learned about fish in the castle?"

I kept a smirk on the inside. The Princess managed to keep her composure. "Well, not exactly." She coughed softly into her hand before continuing. "Helen was supposed to gather my book so that I could spend an afternoon reading. I was sick and my tutor decided if I was going to spend the afternoon in bed, I could finish my book so that we would be ready to start a new one." She glanced at me and I gave her a small smile.

Olympia cut in, throwing a look between myself and the Princess. "Washeen knows what happened, apparently."

"Helen brought the wrong book," I said. "Both covers were green, and so she proceeded to take the one off the tutors desk. It turned out to be a book on all the wildlife in Evergreen."

"My current book was dreadfully boring," Princess Seattel admitted. "This one had interesting facts." She turned to face Sir Coulee. "Have you ever seen a marmot, Sir Coulee?"

"Once," the knight replied, breathing a little heavily from his rowing. "They are quite weird."

"I would love to see them."

"What is a marmot?"

As Princess Seattel explained to Olympia how marmots look like rats, but bigger, I watched as the shore got closer. The river was rushing but was not too wild. The old man said it was an excellent day for crossing. "Would you like me to row, Sir Coulee?" I questioned the man.

"I am fine." The man was slightly red and sweaty, but his eyes darted to Princess Seattel before he glanced at me. If his way of impressing the Princess was to row the boat across the entire river, that was fine by me. I settled back, listening back in on the conversation that the girls were having.

"So you had to learn all about how to sit properly and all that?" Olympia asked Princess Seattel. "I heard that noble ladies even have lessons on how to walk up stairs." She turned and faced me. "Could you imagine! Telling someone to move their feet slower? More 'daintily'?"

Princess Seattel giggled. "It was not that extreme."

"Maybe not for you!" Olympia looked horrified. "If someone tried to teach me how to walk up stairs, I would- well I mean - I would feel like a fopdoodle*!" A mental picture of the princess walking as flamboyantly as the farm girl almost made me lose composure. Even Sir Coulee did a quiet chuckle.

"What do you think they are talking about?" Olympia nudged me. I stumbled in my step a bit, before continuing onward. Up ahead, Princess Seattel was talking with Sir Coulee, who was leading the group. It was evening and the light was slowly falling farther and farther into the trees. The path we were following was clear, so we did not have to cut through brush or climb up hills. Once in a while we would pass another traveling couple or wagon and greetings would be thrown out.

"I am not sure," I replied to the farm girl.

"When Kenne and I took walks, we talked about everything from the sun and moon to family and friends." The girl let out a sigh. "Sometimes, he would recite poetry to me." Once again, my feet stumbled on the path ahead.

"I highly doubt Sir Coulee is reciting poetry," I commented to the girl. Up ahead, the Princess let out a laugh and I narrowed my eyes at the sight. Sir Coulee looked highly impressed with himself and even placed his hand gently on her upper arm.

"Loosen up," Olympia nudged me. "I think it is cute."

"She is the Crown Princess." My voice was curt. "Besides, Sir Coulee is focused on the mission." My words were betrayed, however, when the Princess laughed once again.

Chapter 19

Now that we were farther away from Lone Pine, the path we continued to take south had a few rougher, muddier patches. I kept my focus thinking about Sir Walla organizing the troops. Surely, soon, without a sighting of either the King or the Princess, and with Gems running around the country, the Knight would have the troops begin to take back the state.

Sir Coulee suddenly jolted up his hand, making our small group pause and look ahead. Because of his violent gesture, I gently pushed the Princess behind me and took a step forward. There, next to the path, was a small stream. Two gentlemen were there, filling up canteens of water and chatting away. Both wore muddy and slightly ripped green capes with crests. They were knights.

"Knights of Evergreen!" Olympia breathed. Her eyes were wide and I realized this would be the first time that the farmer girl had seen more than three knights at once. She watched as they popped the lids back onto their containers.

"Sir Quincy and Sir Sumner! " Sir Coulee called to the men, his voice sounding much more enthusiastic than I had ever heard him before. He began to strut forward. The knights turned upon hearing their names.

"Sir Coulee!" the one with black hair spoke, amazed at the sight of seeing his fellow knight in arms. "We were sure that you were lost in the battle of the castle." He placed his canteen on his belt before clasping arms with Sir Coulee. He grinned big.

Sir Coulee chuckled. "I am fine! I was hoping you would be okay, Sir Sumner."

A breeze brushed through the tree and I held back myself from shivering. The sky was a beautiful merge of purples, reds, and oranges. Sir Sumner let out a laugh. "We are better than okay! We actually have some good news!" He opened his mouth to speak but stopped.

This perked my interest, but before anything could be declared, the Princess stepped out from behind me. The knights instantly gasped and knelt, having the Princess in their presence. Their capes fluttered behind them.

"Your majesty!" Sir Sumner breathed out.

The Princess nodded toward the men. "Knights." She stood tall, her chin tipped slightly up. I could tell she felt confident with her hair tied back. It was not her everyday Princess Seattel look, especially with the muddy dress, but in some way it made her even more noble. Even more royal. Even more powerful.

"This is even better news!" Sir Sumner declared, sharing glances with Sir Quincy. "We were traveling on our own for a few days before we ran into another group of knights heading down south."

"Another group?" I questioned. "How many?"

Sir Quincy paused, looking between Sir Coulee and myself. His eyes rested on the Evergreen crest on my shoulder. "And who might you be?" He did not answer the question and I knew it was because he was unsure of my presence. Although everyone knew that Princess Seattel had a personal guard, not many knew of my looks and name unless they were close to the Evergreen royalty.

"Sir Washeen." I nodded politely to the man. "Guard of the Evergreen Princess."

"Pleasure to meet you," Sir Quincy greeted me. He looked more relaxed and did not seem bothered about Olympia's silent presence behind Sir Coulee. Whether it be because she was obviously a peasant, or because she was close to Princess Seattel's side, I do not know. "If you will follow us this way we can bring you to our- I mean your camp."

"Very well." Princess Seattel nodded toward the knight, her hands crossed daintily in front of her. Olympia watched the entire scene unfold, jaw open. I inwardly smirked as the girl had never seen Princess Seattel behave in such a royal manner.

We began to tromp off the path and into brush again, following the two knights through the trees. I followed the Princess two steps behind and to the left as usual. Sir Coulee was extra cautious and would offer his hand to the Princess when there was a bigger step or a fallen tree. I practically scoffed at the gestures, knowing he was only doing this now as there were other knights present. He did not do this on our previous travels.

Sir Sumner led the group, followed by Sir Coulee and Princess Seattel. Olympia followed behind me as I watched the Princess' every move, ready to step in if a situation would come up. Sir Quincy was the last of the group.

Olympia murmured. "I almost forgot that Seattel was the Crown Princess. I can not believe I was traveling with the actual Princess!" Her face was slightly shocked but her cheeks were blushing red and I could tell she loved the entire situation.

A few bushes were chopped, signalizing more than a few people had come this way. "How did you cross the river?" Sir Coulee asked Sir Sumner. The knight turned to the left and the group followed.

"There is another way to cross closer to the Evergreen Palace. Sir Quincy knew about it. It was his father that lent us his boat." Sir Coulee offered his hand once again to the Princess and she took it, smiling graciously at the man. I did not know why I stomped so tense.

We entered a small clearing as dusk was settling in. There were two fires in the clearing ahead, with tents made of blankets and branches set around. At least three dozen men were in the clearing, some eating, some sleeping, and some talking together. Most were soldiers and a few guards from the castle that I recognized. There were four or so other knights.

All of them stopped their conversation when we entered the clearing. A few of them nudged the sleeping men awake. Princess Seattel walked out from the brush behind me and a gasp and muffled hushes went through the men. They all knelt before the Princess before them.

"Rise." Her voice was soft but held authority at the same time. Her hair tie had come undone in the small trek through the woods, yet her figure held power in front of the men.

One of the men spoke up. "We had hoped the rumors of you escaping were true, but we had dared not hope after what happened to the King." A murmur went through the camp and as the knights and soldiers rose many looks were thrown toward Sir Coulee. The knight that spoke up gasped again. "Sir Coulee! There was rumor you were also slain. I am happy to see you are safe." Sir Coulee and the man clasped arms as Princess Seattel spoke.

"Sir..."

"Sir Harring, my Princess," the knight did a quick bow before her. He was an older knight and I did not recognize him either. However, there were many stationed away from the castle whom I have not seen or heard of in a long time. It would make sense that Sir Coulee would know most of these knights. The man had traveled and trained with more of the men than I had even seen. At the same time, it made me feel inferior. I should have studied up on the knights of the kingdom.

"Sir Harring, you spoke of my Father," Princess Seattel reminded the man. I threw a look toward Sir Coulee, who's heart must have been beating as fast as my own. His face was slightly pale and his eyes darted to mine. I turned my head away. "How is he? Was he gravely injured?" There was no thought of death in the Princess' mind.

There was no way Sir Coulee or myself would be able to keep the unfortunate truth from her any longer.

Sir Harring seemed to realize the awkward situation that now was before him. The knight stuttered before glancing between Sir Coulee and myself. I felt slightly bad and embarrassed that the man was put in this situation.

"My Princess," he began, lowering his voice. The other knights and soldiers behind him respected the private moment that they were unwilling part of and turned, forcing themselves to continue to chatter and whittle, a few cooking some food. Eyes did, however, dart our way.

Princess Seattel let out a small huff as a feeling of dread settled in her bones. She looked between Sir Coulee and myself. Sir Coulee refused to meet her eyes and simply gave me a small glance. "Wait," her voice shook. "The King is down south with the troops." She took a step toward me and placed her hand on my arm. "He is."

I could feel the gaze of Sir Coulee burn into my arm where the Princess' hand rested. I resisted the urge to place my hand on top of hers. At the same time, her hand sat heavily and I felt in the wrong.

Sir Harring cleared his throat. "Princess Seattel, the King is dead."

Whether the entire world went silent at that time, or whether it was simply my hearing selecting what it truly wanted to hear, a deep gasp came from the Princess in front of me. Her crystal eyes did not move from mine and neither did her hand. They were bright and seemed to pierce my soul. I suddenly felt something I had not in a long time.

Guilt.

I should have told her.

I could not look away.

Sir Coulee refused to look at anything except his feet. Olympia sat herself down on a log with tears rolling down her cheeks over a man that she had only heard of. Princess Seattel moved from me to Sir Coulee. The lack of her hand on my arm sent goose bumps up my arm from the cold. She placed a finger on his chin and raised his face to meet her eyes. "Sir Coulee? He is down south."

"The King is dead," the knight before her softly spoke.

The wind calmly went through the area, gently brushing back the chopped hair of the future Queen before us. Her face was still calm, but a fierce rage was growing within her. I could tell by the lightning suddenly snapping around her crystal eyes that were filling with liquid. Some drops of water fell from the sky as the Princess' mood seemed to be reflected in the area around us.

"You told me he was in the south." The voice was curt and sharp and inwardly I winced, relieved the tone was not directed at me.

"It was not an intentional lie," Sir Coulee told the Princess.

"You told me!" Her voice raised a notch. "While we were collecting firewood." She yanked her hand off his arm. "You assured me," she said through clenched teeth. "How was that not intentional?"

One thing you do not do, is make a fool of Princess Seattel. I glared at the man before me. I did not know that Sir Coulee lied to the Princess' face. If I had known, I could have changed this outcome. How dare he!

"And I believed you," she hissed at the man. "You said he is not dead. You told me!" Her voice rose into a scream and the man before her cowered.

"It was the best answer at the time," Sir Coulee defended his actions.

"Your Majesty," I spat out toward the man, furious that he did not use her title. Had I been asked straightforwardly by the Princess where her father was, there would be no lies. Sir Coulee was a liar.

"It was the best answer at the time, your Majesty," Sir Coulee revamped his answer.

Princess Seattel raised her head and the man in front of her could tell he was in trouble. He knelt before her. I ignored his desperate sneaked look at me and focused on my only task before me.

The Princess.

Olympia was behind the Princess and as she put her arm out to touch her, I held my hand out and shook my head. Sir Harring dared only to breathe and even the men in the background stopped speaking, glancing once in a while at the scene that was taking place.

"You openly admit to lying to the Princess of the Evergreen? I could have you stripped of your title," she hissed again. That was the least she could do, and he knew that.

"Yes, your Majesty."

"And you!" And suddenly I was under the same scorching look that Sir Coulee before me was. Although not guilty of the lies, it was clear that I could have informed the Princess sooner of her fathers death. I felt ice in my core and the withering look she gave me hurt more than words can explain. I bowed my head and did not meet her eyes as she glared me down.

"If Sir Coulee did not tell me, I would expect that someone who had worked beside me for so long would have informed me of the truth." I knew she could not call me a friend, but that was the point she was making. How deep the betrayal went.

There was not a sign of my Princess I knew in front of me. There was only an ice cold Queen.

I went down on my knees also. "My Princess, I -" But no more words made their way out of my mouth. I was interrupted.

"It is my fault only, your Majesty," Sir Coulee spoke up. "I ordered Sir Washeen not to speak of the matter with you."

"He does not take orders from you," Princess Seattel seethed toward the knight. Another gust of wind went through the area and I felt the chills hit my bones.

"He only found out two days ago, your Majesty," Sir Coulee spoke up again. I could not help but marvel at the braveness of the knight on his knees. "I informed him before we reached Lone Pine."

I dared to take a look at the Princess before me and breathed a little easier when her anger was directed back at the knight. I did not expect Sir Coulee taking the blame off me. Although, now I have a little more respect for the man. "Get out of my sight," the Princess hissed at him. "I never want to lay eyes on you again."

Olympia let out a little gasp and covered her mouth with her hand, tears flowing down her cheeks. The situation was tense. Sir Harring stood straighter. Sir Coulee arose from his knees and bowed before the Princess. "Thank you, your Majesty." He did not lose his title. Nor did he lose any limbs.

"You may continue with us to the Beaverlands," she spoke in a voice so low, you had to strain to hear it, "but I do not want you to get in my way. Once we reach Sunnyside Castle, you will be posted far away from the castle." She did a sharp turn and walked into some of the brush behind her, escaping the looks of the men in the camp behind her.

Sir Coulee took a quick breath. I quickly stood as well and followed the Princess into the woods. Whether or not she liked it, I was her personal body guard and unless she dismissed me, as Queen, I would remain by her, put there by the King himself.

I thought about the reasons for Princess Seattel to continue to travel with Sir Coulee. He was one of the hero's who had defeated the Gems in the past, and she could really use as many knights as she could get right now. Although, not stripping him of his title was the most gracious thing I had known her to do. Another bonus was that he knew the knights of the group and trusted them. Princess Seattel relied on him in the past and now she can rely on these men.

The sobs came quickly once she was away from the camp and in her own privacy. She sat on a log and the tears were coming faster than her sleeves could keep up with. I stood beneath a nearby tree and listened for danger close by. She turned and noticed my presence.

"Go away, Sir Washeen."

I held my ground. "I was made your bodyguard by the King. I cannot."

"He is dead!" All royal behavior was gone as the Princess shouted at me. "You can go! I want you to leave! I just want to mourn by myself," she sniffed. She sobbed into her sleeve once again.

I, however, refused to take a step. "Until you are made Queen to hold the same rank as the King who commanded me, I cannot."

"GET OUT OF HERE!" I had never heard a scream echo out of her like that, the devastation in her voice. I forced myself to remain as I usually did. Hand on the hilt of my sword. Face emotionless. "LEAVE!" Princess Seattel yelled a few more times, but seeing that I would not move, and finally accepting my being there, she turned around and cried the other way so that I would not be in her line of vision. My insides felt shredded. It hurt. I swallowed hard and blinked fast.

She cried for many moments. I titled my head as the sound of a twig snapping came from nearby. The Princess seemed not to hear it, nor see the golden haired head pop out of the brush. Olympia motioned at me. I took a step to the left and crouched down to hear what the girl had to say. "Go over there!"

"I am guarding," I whispered back as quietly as I could. "I am the guard of the Princess."

Olympia rolled her eyes. "I know that!" she whispered back. "I am saying go comfort her!"

"It is not my job," I reminded the farmer girl. I did not want to get yelled at.

Olympia sighed and I glanced at the Princess, making sure she did not hear. After all, she did want to be alone. "Remember our talk?" Olympia hissed. "Be her friend. Be there for her."

"She shouted at me to leave," I informed the girl. "She does not want me comforting her right now."

"It does not hurt to try," Olympia quietly said back. "Just try." And with that, the girl disappeared into the brush, going more softly than she came. The wind blew through the area and I felt the cold hit my bones once again. If I was feeling it, so was the Princess.

I stood from my crouched position and slowly took a few steps in the direction of the girl. Did I dare? What if she would yell at me again? My thoughts were interrupted by a particularly loud sob that shook Princess Seattel's shoulders. The decision was made.

I cautiously approached her from the side. She did not acknowledge me, her head down in her arms. I lowered myself on the log beside her, close enough that she knew I had sat. Her crystal eyes peered up for a second and I took a moment to wipe her crooked hair off her wet cheek and place it behind her ear. There was no action by the Princess so I slowly took off my jacket and laid it over her shoulders. I felt the cold bite me quickly but I ignored it, placing my arm on top of the jacket that was now around her, pressing the warm fabric into her own cold skin.

She scooted closer and placed her hand on top of my knee. It was shaking and pale from the cold. I gently placed my other hand on top. And although the crying continued, I could tell the grief was not consuming her. I said nothing, simply sitting myself next to her. I could feel the cold of her skin, the wet tears that sometimes landed on my knee, and something move in my heart.

Chapter 20

A small crack was heard to our right as we sat there. I stood and moved back to my spot by the tree. Sir Harring stumbled into the scene, bowing toward the Princess on the log. The Princess had dried her tears and the only sign of her sadness was her pale face. My jacket remained on her shoulders, the only hint that I had been there.

"Princess Seattel," he addressed her, "we have set up a tent in the clearing and are settling down for the night." The Princess looked up and around at her surroundings as if noticing for the first time that the forest had darkened around her. "If we continue our walking tomorrow, we should reach the south and the border of Beaverland in four days at the most."

"Very good." She slowly rose from the log and motioned for the knight to lead her back to camp. The man did a slight bow before turning and heading back through the brush. I followed the Princess a few steps behind her. We entered the clearing and the tent that the knight had spoken of was simply a few

blankets hung in a square formation from the trees. Nonetheless, I was pleased they had done something for her privacy.

The Princess stood before the men, the tears gone and the
blood flowing back to her face, making her cheeks rosy once
again. A few men were already settled down for the night, while
others were adding wood to the three fires in the clearing. The
one closest to the 'tent' was the biggest. A warm, tasty smell
filled the area.

"Get a good sleep, men," she spoke strongly. "We will continue moving south in the morning." A few men let out some cele-
bration sounds and others turned and continued their conversations. She turned to go into the tent but was stopped by Sir
Sumner, holding a simmering bowl of stew.

"No, thank you," Princess Seattel politely responded to the
knight before her. "I am not hungry." As she pulled aside one
of the blankets of the tent, a movement caught her eye and
she made eye contact with Sir Coulee for a split second. Her
face went emotionless and she turned, disappearing into the
tent. Olympia gave me a smile from her place by one of the
fires, stirring a cooking pot with a giant wooden spoon. A few
men were lined up with bowls of bark, waiting for their portion,
including Sir Coulee. He refused to look anyone in the eye.

I took the bowl from Sir Harring and followed the Princess
into the tent. There was a cleared area on the ground of all
brush and sticks, with two blankets set up and something that
resembled a pillow.

Although her dress was covered in mud and rips from the adventures we had just gone through, the Princess of the Evergreen sat on the bed and sighed, looking down at her hands. My jacket was still over her shoulders, even though now there was a warm, crackling fire right outside.

I placed the stew on her lap and ignored the small noise of protest she made. "You need to eat this." She simply looked at me, then the food, and then began picking what I believe were pieces of carrot out of the mix.

"Thank you, Sir Washeen." Satisfied she would at least stomach some of the food, I let her have her privacy and exited the tent, making sure that the area was secure before heading off to Olympia to receive some food of my own.

As I approached, I heard the conversation happening between Sir Quincy and Sir Coulee. "It is a good thing we decided to stop for food when we did," the knight was telling his fellow man in arms. "Otherwise we would have never found you."

"We were walking along the path there, hoping to find some sort of trader or merchant to give us some food and supplies for the journey," Sir Sumner added in. "We had gotten a few supplies from the last town but with a group like this," he motioned around to the three or four dozen men around him, "food is eaten quick."

Sir Coulee nodded, poking at his own food. "That was a stroke of luck."

I was distracted from the conversation as Olympia plopped some of the stew onto a clean piece of bark in my hands. "Here you are, Sir Washeen."

"Thank you, Olympia," I nodded at the girl before me. "So they nominated you as cook?"

Olympia let out a laugh. "Actually, I volunteered. I was watching a few of these men try to chop some of the carrots and I walked over and took the knives out of their hands!" A few men around her, although with smiles on their faces, tried to protest that this happened. "I figured the last thing we needed was someone to chop off their own fingers!" She pointed the wooden spoon at a few of the men cackling at the other men's expense. "But at least they were trying, unlike some of you!"

I could tell that the men enjoyed the spirit that Olympia brought to the place. They laughed and shoved each other in agreement, all the while eating the delicious smelling stew that she had made. "You know," I began, changing the conversation, "Princess Seattel would not mind you bunking with her."

The farmer girl looked at a blanket next to her and then at the group of men who were watching her intently. "That does sound like a better solution than sleeping in the midst of that," and once again she pointed the wooden spoon at the men.

"I have room next to me!" one of the men piped up, lifting the corner of his blanket. The other men whistled and laughed. I cringed inwardly at the behavior. But alas, they were simply guards from the palace. What would you expect?

"Now, Moxee," Olympia spoke louder. "What would your wife say about that behavior?"

"I do not have a wife," he admitted.

"And now you know why," she told him. "But I am sorry to ruin your dreams, I am already betrothed." I ignored the stab of guilt to my stomach. She turned back to me and smiled, but I could see that she was happy with my suggestion. "I will finish serving here and then go to Seattel." I retreated from the fire and took a seat by Sir Sumner, Sir Quincy, and Sir Coulee on the log. I kept a close eye on the tent, making sure no one would enter. Sir Harring was currently patrolling the area.

"The south is just a short journey. A few days at most," Sir Sumner spoke, having a small map on his knees. He traced the route we were to take with his pointer finger. I raised my eyebrow. Updated maps were very rare and most of them resided in the castle, used during council meetings. I was impressed that he would own one. It would have cost a lot of coin. Even the forests were painted green.

Sir Coulee stretched his arms and yawned, although I could tell it was mainly for show. "I think I will retire for the night," he informed his fellow knights. He made eye contact with me but quickly retreated to a quiet spot in the clearing, placing his blanket down by other slumbering men.

I inhaled the food. Although hot, it was delicious as I had not eaten anything in a while. I checked on the Princess once I was done, finding her already asleep and Olympia laying next to her. Her bowl was not empty, but missing a few chunks of the stew that were previously there. The fires were dying and so I added a couple logs. Sir Harring approached me as I did so.

"Sir Quincy and Sir Sumner have the first watch," he informed me. "A few guards and Sir Zillah are doing second," he motioned to the one knight I was unfamiliar with, "and Sir Coulee and I are doing third." He turned. "You are free to sleep the night."

"That is very gracious," I nodded at the knight in front of me, who took the role of head knight over this group. "I will sleep next to the Princess' tent. Wake me if there are any concerns." I laid my blanket down and settled in as comfortably as the ground would allow. I would like to say it took many long hours before I felt safe enough to slumber, but in reality, it was mere moments.

The next morning came as quickly as the fall after summer. The camp was aroused early and breakfast was cooked. This time Olympia had orchestrated a few soldiers to cook with her, making it go faster. I was not sure who was on hunting duty this morning, but the pile of rabbits and squirrels being cooked was impressive. Princess Seattel was yet to leave her tent, although I did check in on her and found her trying to wash her face and arms. My jacket was nicely put by the 'door' of the tent and I picked it up, putting it back on.

Blankets were rolled and packs were carried and in a few moments the camp was ready to depart. Princess Seattel looked over the map with Sir Harring and Sir Sumner, who showed her a village or two we would travel through.

"What are some resources that we are in need of?" the Princess questioned the head knight.

"Currently, as we are following the river down south, water is not a problem. We seem to have enough blankets and clothes for the men, although I am sure you would like a clean dress." Princess Seattel simply looked at the man and he stammered to continue. "I would say food is always going to be a high need, although we have been locating many edible plants and animals here in the woods."

Sir Quincy walked up to the group. "The men are ready to go."

"Let us move," the Princess declared. Sir Harring did a slight bow before turning to the men, bellowing instructions. Princess Seattel turned sharply to pick up her own pack and almost walked straight into Sir Coulee. He was holding out her pack for her, but not meeting her eyes. After a quick intake of breath, the Princess snatched the bag out of his hands and turned back to face me.

"You will be guarding me, Sir Washeen?"

"Of course, your majesty." I did a quick bow.

"Sir Coulee is not to get within close proximity of me again." With the curt tone, the Princess stomped forward behind Sir Harring and Sir Zillah. I marched ahead as well, staying within close range but giving her space as well. What was Sir Coulee thinking? Did he want to be exiled?

The rest of the men followed suit and Olympia ran forward to walk behind me. She was carrying just a blanket in a pack and had a stumbling Moxee to her left, carrying more than what the average pack should have weighed. I said nothing, although I applauded the girl in my head for making the man work.

We walked for many hours. There was a short stop for lunch, which mainly consisted of leftover cooked rabbit and squirrel from morning breakfast and some wild blueberries.

"I am sorry I did not suggest this before," Princess Seattel said to Olympia while snacking on some berries, "but if you would like, I could spare two guards to escort you back home. I am sure Kenne is worried sick and you would probably like to get home."

Olympia shrugged. "That is kind of you to offer, Seattel," she began. Sir Harring stumbled past, so shocked by the informalities laid out before him that he forgot to watch where his feet were taking him. "But I am sure that Kenne would understand that this mission of yours is much more important than me coming home." I swallowed hard, as the girl thought of her betrothed waiting for her. "I will continue with you to the south."

Princess Seattel smiled and placed her hand on the farmer girl's arm. "That is very noble, Olympia." She stood up and stretched and I quickly placed the rest of the rabbit meat into my mouth, wiping my hands on my trousers. It was a sunny day, the rain seeming to be gone for a while, with blue skies above. Spring was half way over and the nicer weather was bound to come soon.

We continued our walk. Chatter happened here and there and a few of the men played verbal games and spoke some riddles as they walked. Our road was not busy, with a few travelers crossing paths with us. Many were on their normal routes, while a few spoke horror stories of escaping the Gems farther north. One family had two little kids and the little girl would not stop crying. Her older brother had been killed while the family fled for their lives.

Princess Seattel located some of the cooked rabbit from our food supply and gave it to the family. They were grateful. "Long live the Queen," the father praised the Princess.

"I am not Queen," she reminded the man.

"But you will be, and that gives us all a great hope," the man beamed at her. Him and his family continued their journey with us for an hour or so, before turning down another path toward a town his sister dwelled in.

It was another hour or so before another crossroads was met. "Which way from here, Sir Harring," Princess Seattel asked the head knight before her. The man had the map out and was studying it, his forehead wrinkled as he identified the small roads on the paper.

"I believe we go left," he stated.

Sir Coulee made a small noise, enough to have me turn and look at the man. He caught my eye and slowly shook his head, disagreeing with the head knight. I pretended to ignore the liar, but his action did catch my attention and I tuned into the conversation.

"I am not sure," Sir Sumner spoke up, disagreeing with Sir Harring. "I remember the name of this town. I believe when we were fighting the Gems months ago in the east, it was brought up. One of the knights had a previous mission in Krupp and he had stated that it had not gone well. Apparently the village is full of looters and thieves, tricking those who step foot into their town. It is quite dangerous."

"Nonsense!" Sir Zillah denied. "Surely such a village would not exist in the Evergreen Kingdom?" He turned toward the Princess for some confirmation.

Princess Seattel studied the map and then looked at the few knights around her. "My father never mentioned this place, nor had I heard of it in any council meeting." She turned and faced Sir Sumner. "Are you positive this is the town that the knight spoke of?"

"It was many months ago and he spoke of it in passing," Sir Sumner confessed. "My memory could be off. Sir Coulee-" his voice drifted off as his eyes met the stern look of the Princess' face. "Perhaps someone else who was with me in the east would remember the conversation better than myself."

The man was suggesting Sir Coulee and there was no denying it. Princess Seattel refused to even look the knight's way. "I say that we head through it and see if we can trade for some more food and supplies," she decided. "If Sir Sumner cannot fully remember, it may be a different town than what he thinks." The group picked up their packs they had placed down and got to their feet.

Sir Harring took a left down the path. I glanced back at Sir Coulee, who once again shook his head at me. I felt an uncomfortable breeze hit my bones and in the back of my mind I knew that this was the town of thieves and looters that Sir Sumner had mentioned.

If only Sir Coulee could confirm it.

Chapter 21

The group had barely taken a few steps down the path to Krupp when out of the corner of my eye I saw Sir Coulee suddenly walk forward toward the Princess. From her warning earlier, I intervened and placed myself between her and the knight. He tried to go around, and I sidestepped, blocking his path.

When he tried once again, placing his hands on my shoulder and pushing me slightly, I knew I had to take stronger action. "Move aside, Sir Washeen."

I pushed back. The man did not want to move, even pushing me once more, and so I unsheathed my sword and placed it between our bodies. "Step back, Sir Coulee. This is the last warning. The Princess does not want you close to her." I had no intention of striking the man and the sword was merely placed there to show I take the duty of guarding the Princess seriously.

He put his hands up, realizing his mistake by touching me. He tried to reason. "Listen, Sir Washeen, I need to talk to Princess Seattel." I believed he truly did have something important to say, as it was apparent in his eyes. However, I had received orders from Princess Seattel that he was not to approach her.

"The Princess does not want to see you." At this point, the group had stopped moving, and trying not to stare at the scene, some men mumbled among themselves. Princess Seattel dropped her conversation with Sir Harring and the man quickly folded the map up.

The Princess spoke with her back turned. "Leave, Sir Coulee."

"Surely if he has something that important to say, you can let him talk to Seattel," Olympia stepped up beside us. She motioned toward the Princess who was looking our way, a few steps to the side of us. "She can hear what he has to say." Sir Harring forced his jaw closed at the lack of formalities the farmer girl continued to give the future Queen.

"I was ordered not to let him close." I stared at the knight in front of me, jaw tilted up and firm. His eyes hit the ground.

Olympia huffed. "Washeen, this is ridiculous." Olympia grabbed Sir Coulee's arm and tried to tug him around me. I blocked the path once again, giving the farmer's girl a slight push out of the way with my shoulder while using the point of my sword to back Sir Coulee away the few steps he advanced. He held his hands up once again when the point lightly jabbed his chest. "Washeen!" Olympia spoke up, flabbergasted at my actions. "Simply let him speak."

"No." I planted my feet firm and the knight before me knew I meant what I had said. He took a step back.

"Seattel!" And before I could stop her, the farmer girl caught the attention of the Princess by speaking up and waving her hands toward her. "Coulee obviously has something extremely important to tell you. He knows he is supposed to stay away. He knows you could take away his title, but yet he is trying to talk to you." Princess Seattel raised her head and turned away from the group.

"I do not wish to see him."

"But he needs to tell you something!" the blonde haired girl urged the Princess of the Evergreen Kingdom. Princess Seattel turned her head away from the scene. Olympia grabbed her arm. The forest seemed too quiet as the soldiers and knights could not believe this girl would touch the Princess without permission. "Tell Washeen to let him go!" I narrowed my eyes at the sight of her hand squeezing Princess Seattel's arm, but decided Sir Coulee would be doing more damage if he were to approach. I continued to hold him at sword point.

The next action caused shock to go throughout the group as the Princess forcefully yanked her arm away from Olympia. "I will not see that liar," she hissed, her face twisted in anger. Olympia, shocked, looked down at her hand as if she could not believe what just happened. A determined look came over her face and once again, before I could act, she grabbed the Princess' arm once again. This time, the men did not stay quiet and gasped at the action.

"Do not touch me!" The words forced me to change plans and I reached the Princess' side, ripping Olympia's hand off her arm and placing the farm girl at the tip of my sword instead, forcing her to take a few steps back from the royal.

Strangely enough, it did not stop the girl in her actions. Instead of trying to touch the Princess again, Olympia continued her arguing, ignoring the poke of my steel. "You are being unreasonable! He may have lied to you, but his information could still come in handy."

"How am I supposed to trust him?" Princess Seattel asked the girl before her. "He could leave out important information that I would need." The words were directed and hit deep on the knight and his eyes hit the ground once again. Although, they did not stay there long, as Olympia argued his case and he raised them to watch the action.

"Maybe he was just doing what he thought was best." She took a step forward and jutted her chin, ignoring the poke of my blade on her midsection.

"He did not think I could handle the news." The Princess stepped out from behind me and now was at my side.

"Maybe he was right. You are not doing so well now. Look how bitter you are. I do not blame him for not telling you." I did not know Olympia was capable of taking such tones.

"He is to stay out of my way!" It was not a suggestion that the Princess was making. It was an order.

Olympia threw her hands up. "You are acting like a child!"

The forest went silent once again. I swear I heard some of the men blink. Then, there was a pause as Princess Seattel had no remark to throw back at the girl. She looked around at the soldiers and knights watching with wide eyes and sensing her discomfort at the publicity of it all. I narrowed my eyes at Olympia. How dare she act disrespectful to the future Queen in front of her men! I gripped the hilt tighter.

Sir Harring cleared his throat. "Take a moment, men."

They scattered like flies, a few heading back the way we came while others disappeared in the bushes, speaking about finding more wild berries or what they wanted to catch for dinner. The only ones to remain were Sir Coulee, Sir Sumner, Sir Harring, Olympia, the Princess, and myself.

"Perhaps we need a moment to calm ourselves," Sir Harring spoke again, raising his hands and coming between the infuriated Olympia and the seething Princess. "Shall we take a breath?"

I did not relax my position and every now and then darted my eyes to Sir Coulee who now stood behind the fiery farmer girl. The atmosphere was tense. "I have not finished what I wish to say," Olympia stated.

"I believe you have." Princess Seattel's voice was curt and direct.

Olympia took a new approach, speaking with me instead of the Princess to my side. "Washeen, you know what Coulee has to say is important. Otherwise, he would stay out of Seattel's

way. Why would he risk so much to give her useless information?" Her tone turned to one of desperation. Her eyes met
mine, begging me, and although I knew there was reason in
what she was saying, I had to follow my Princess' command. I
did not speak. I held my position.

Sir Coulee could tell that there was no way a civil discussion
could happen now. He placed his hand on Olympia's shoulder.
"The Princess has given a command." But to his surprise, the
girl shrugged his hand off and continued to speak.

"Who is her adviser?" The question caught us all off guard
for a second. Olympia looked around the group as we all sent
small glances to each other. Who was her adviser? "Well?" the
girl pushed. I figured it would be the same one her father had.
However, where he was, was a mystery in itself.

"I do not need one," was Princess Seattel's answer. She folded her arms across her chest.

"Yes, you do." There was no question in the farmer girl's
voice. Olympia took a step forward and I released some of the
pressure off the blade so as not to hurt her. "Then I declare
myself her adviser. And as Adviser, I advise you to listen to what
Coulee has to say." The end of her sentence wavered, yet she
held her ground.

Sir Sumner let out a chuckle. "You cannot do that." He nervously looked around the group but received no confirmation
of his statement. We all continued to stare at her. "Can she?"

Sir Harring let out a huff. "Of course not. Advisers are well trained, noblemen, and own land of their own." He motioned toward the farmer girl. "She has none of these traits." I was not about to speak up, but technically she did own some land in her village.

Olympia seemed to completely ignore the two knights, repeating her previous words. "As your Adviser, I highly recommend you listen to what Sir Coulee has to say." I raised my eyebrow at the use of a title, but held my ground until the Princess would speak. The knight from the east stood tall behind the farmer girl, ready to speak when spoken too.

Shocking a knight was not an easy mission to accomplish, however, Olympia seemed to do just that as Princess Seattel put her hand up and then down, signaling I could drop my sword. I sheathed it as she spoke. "Very well, Adviser. Sir Coulee, what is this matter you wish to speak of?" She crossed her arms and stared down the knight before her.

At this bizarre situation, Sir Harring's mouth dropped open, but the knight managed his surprise well and closed it quickly. Sir Sumner shifted his feet and sent a very confused look my way, but I refused to acknowledge it.

Sir Coulee stepped forward and knelt before Princess Seattel. "We should not travel to Krupp, your highness."

"Why not?"

Sir Coulee continued, his head bowed. "Sir Sumner's memory was correct in stating that it is a village full of thieves and looters. I also had heard stories from that particular knight that it is not a place for women to travel." He raised his head and met her eyes. "He spoke of some unthinkable things happening there."

Princess Seattel did not let the words faze her to the untrained eye, but I could see her posture stiffen slightly as she imagined what these things could be. Olympia noticeably gulped behind Sir Coulee. "I thank you for telling me this. Sir Harring," she addressed the other knight.

"Yes, your majesty?" There was a tense silence as the same thought went through everyone's mind. Would she listen to the man?

"Open the map. Let us plan a new route."

"You cannot do something like that ever again," Sir Coulee scolded the girl next to him. Olympia seemed not to fret at his words as they continued to walk in step with the rest of the group. I was a few steps to the side and a few steps behind the Princess, who was discussing more plans with the head knight. Her dress was still mud covered but as we walked in the sun, she did not shiver. I made a mental note to see if I could find an extra shirt and trousers for her to wear tonight.

"It worked, did it not?" She beamed at the knight. "And now I am an Adviser!"

"Especially in front of all her men!" The knight shook his head in disbelief. "It was not proper."

"She should listen to you," the girl argued in his defense. "You are a very respected knight and have a lot of good information and plans to assist her with."

"It does not matter," Sir Coulee tried to reason with Olympia. "She is the Crown Princess and what she orders, you do. It is not for us to question her orders."

"But you knew that place was not safe for her! You are saying you would have let her walk in there without speaking to her because she demanded you not?"

"That is exactly what I am saying," the knight informed her. They took a larger step over a mud puddle that was slowly drying in the late afternoon sun. The woods were full of wildlife coming out of their homes to enjoy the sun and I knew supper tonight would be an easy hunt.

Their tones lowered and I strained to hear what was said, all the while keeping an ear to the conversation that the Princess and Sir Harring were having. "How could she just order you to stay away from her?" Olympia asked the knight. "I know she cares for you." My heart skipped a few beats as the memories of the Princess giggling with the knight came back to my mind. "I could never do that to Kenne."

All hopes of Sir Coulee not knowing I was eavesdropping were thrown out of a window as he sharply looked my way and made eye contact with me. I quickly looked ahead at the Princess where my attention was supposed to be. Yet, the knight said nothing of her deceased betrothed. "She does not feel that way about me," the knight told the farmer girl.

Olympia nudged the knight in a friendly way, causing him to take a step to the left before settling back on the normal rhythm of his walking. "I have my suspicions."

"What do you mean by that?" I was startled at how eager the knight had sounded. Before this conversation could be continued, the Princess stepped on a fallen tree, thanks to the help of Sir Harring.

"Knights and soldiers," she spoke loud and clear, "we will settle down here for the night. There is a clearing beyond those bushes." As she motioned, Sir Sumner appeared out from one, obviously scouting the area. "There is about an hour of sun left in the day and so Sir Quincy is going to take a hunting group out for dinner. We need some volunteers." A few men put their hands up and Princess Seattel pointed at five of them. "We need three men to gather wood for the fires tonight and the rest can clear the area and fill the water canteens." I put my arm out and the Princess nodded her thanks at me for the assistance I offered, taking it and stepping off the higher platform.

The soldiers and knights all began to move around, everyone keeping busy and doing the tasks that needed to be done. I followed the Princess through the camp. She stopped next to Olympia.

"Adviser Olympia," she called the girl.

"Yes?" I could almost flinch at the lack of title at the end of that sentence.

"Do you mind being in charge of the dinner tonight, once again?"

Olympia did a nod and excitement filled her face. "It would be my pleasure." Almost without a beat, the girl turned and began to bellow. "Quincy! Moxee! You are on chopping duty!" She took the wooden spoon out of her pack and shoved it into another man's hand and then began ordering the fourth to make a fire.

Princess Seattel took a step back from the scene, a slight smile on her face.

"If I may, your majesty?" I addressed the Princess.

She turned to me. "Yes, Sir Washeen?"

I turned back to the crazy scene around us, men running here and there, Olympia's orders flying around the camp, a few knights looking over the map, and the blankets being hung for the Princess' tent. I stood straight. "I approve of your Adviser."

Her lips rose a touch and for a moment I saw a glimpse of the old Princess Seattel that I would guard in the palace. "I have a feeling I will not regret that decision."

Chapter 22

The next morning and lunch went by as quick as a breeze. We traveled farther south and after we stopped for lunch, Sir Harring announced we were about half way done with our travels. A cheer went up among the men.

It was later that evening that we hit another group of soldiers heading south. They were being led by the famous knight, Sir Marhys, owning one of the richest villages in the entirety of the Evergreen Kingdom, Marysville. Sir Coulee watched every movement of the knight with hero- worshiping eyes and I could not help but smirk at the sight.

Princess Seattel was more than happy to see the knight and his group of men, which was around three times the size of what we were traveling with already. The aged knight had his right to retire from his duties, but the man claimed he would rot away without the adventure. Despite his experience and expertise in the army, Princess Seattel declared that Sir Harring would remain the head knight of the group. Our group now consisted of one hundred and fifty men. Even with the extra hunters scavenging the woods, supper portions were still smaller.

Olympia cooked and chopped food beside one fire while Moxee was appointed the cook of the fire next to her. There were a few jabs going back and forth between them and I realized that they were having a cooking competition amongst the two of them on who could make the tastier food.

I stood with my bowl and Princess Seattel's bowl beside Olympia's fire, waiting my turn to receive dinner. Once the stew was placed in the bowls, I weaved my way through all the men and into the Princess' tent, which had now grown in size. A few knights were inside with the Princess, all studying the map. Surprisingly, Sir Coulee was among them.

"Tomorrow we will enter the desert portion of our journey," Sir Harring was showing the group, "but by nightfall I expect us to be back into the woods." His finger traced something on the map and the other knights nodded in agreement. "The next three days we should travel down this way," his finger slid along, "and reach the south and the Beaverlands by the fourth nightfall."

Sir Coulee spoke up and pointed to a spot on the map. "I have heard that bandits wait in this spot to jump travelers." He motioned to the outside of the tent. "However, with the amount of men we are traveling with, we should have no prob-lems." I watched the Princess closely as the man spoke and was surprised to see that she was listening to what he was saying. However, even though her eyes flickered toward him, she did not address the knight and turned toward Sir Sumner.

"Have the men fill their canteens at the river tomorrow morning before we leave and see to it that the horses are well watered."

"It shall be done." The black haired man bowed toward the Princess and left the tent.

The other knights bowed and also went out of the tent. I remained and handed the bowl of steaming soup toward Princess Seattel. She accepted it and sat on her blanket. I took my place a few feet away, sitting on a patch of grass. We ate in a comfortable silence, the sound of the men happily reuniting with some of their fellow castle guards filling the air.

"What do you think about Sir Coulee?" The question cut the silence and I swallowed my food, looking up at the Princess. Her crystal eyes pierced mine, awaiting my answer. My heart beat faster.

"His actions or himself as a person, Princess?" I replied, toning on the cautious side. There are many different thoughts I had about Sir Coulee and I would prefer to know exactly what the Princess was trying to get at.

"Overall." She continued to watch me closely. I took another bite of food before responding.

"He is a great knight."

"I did not ask you to state the obvious," she huffed. "What do you think of the man?" She took another sip from her canteen. "I am asking for your opinion."

There were many different opinions that I had on Sir Coulee. On the one hand, I found him slightly arrogant. On the other, a respectful knight. I decided to question the Princess back. "Are you wondering if you did the right thing by letting him speak?"

She nodded toward me. "That is one of the reasons I am wondering. Although Olympia assures me it was."

"And the other?"

The Princess took a deep sigh and put her bowl to the side, the remaining food still slightly steaming. "Sir Harring brought up an excellent point today." I thought back to the journey that we made today but could not remember any conversation between the two of them about Sir Coulee. There were a few times I was out of hearing range of the Princess, however, as she was constantly surrounded by three or so knights and there was no dire need for me to follow her as closely as usual. "He pointed out that if anything should happen to me while we battle the Gems, I would have no heir to the throne. I would not be on the front lines, but in war it is impossible to predict the outcome." Her eyes snapped back to mine.

"So you are wondering if Sir Coulee is a good fit for a king." The shock of the statement settled in my bones. My mind slowly began to piece together the thoughts of the Princess. As she will be crowned Queen in the south in a few days, it was not unreasonable for her to think about heirs and a partner to sit next to her on the throne.

"Am I insane?" Princess Seattel suddenly stood and began to pace in the tent. "I spoke to Olympia today as well and she assured me again that Sir Coulee only withheld the truth of my Father's death for my benefit." She let out an exasperated laugh and ran a hand through her hair. There was a smudge of dirt close to her ear. "And although only a few days ago I refused to talk to the man, here I am considering if he would be a good Crown King." She turned back toward me. "Who else am I supposed to consider for the position?"

My mind raced as I tried to process the conversation before me. Princess Seattel marrying Sir Coulee would make him Crown King, meaning that if she were to die, he would take over the kingdom. If they had a child together, that child would rule instead of him. It was not a rule that she must have a Crown King, but it was very responsible of her to think about it as if she did not, the kingdom could fall to untrustworthy hands. "It is not an easy decision to make, your majesty," I slowly said.

She watched me carefully and I kept my face emotionless. "I am asking you your opinion, Washeen. As a friend."

The silence was the most deafening and tense that we had ever had between us. I cleared my throat before speaking, putting down my own dish. "King Yakima, may he rest in peace, spoke his approval of Sir Coulee the night before the castle fell." My eyes met the Princess and she searched mine for more of a hint on my thoughts and feelings. I held them back.

"Very well," she finally spoke. Her eyes did not leave mine for a few moments and I begged her not to speak again, knowing it was not my opinion that I had stated.

Finally, Princess Seattel returned to her seat on her blanket. The conversation started up once again, but thankfully, this time the topic had changed.

"Sir Marhys mentioned his group had heard rumors of another group heading south. At least a hundred men or so." She took a gulp out of her canteen. "Sir Harring believes there are at least seven thousand men awaiting our arrival, a third of that cavalry." She took another bite. "With our troops organized and perhaps some help from Prince Eugene we should be able to retake the kingdom easily." Her jaw clenched. "Those Gem brutes are scattered, each one greedy to help themselves rather than to function like an army." I had heard most of the discussions between her and the knights and I know she was simply saying these things to reassure herself. However, she could save her words as I did not need convincing. I believe we will win our kingdom back.

"Long will last the Evergreen Kingdom," I agreed.

Her eyes hit mine. There was a moment of silence. "Long will last."

The next few days went slowly by. With each step getting closer to the Beaverland, the conversations of the men picked up in energy and happiness, despite traveling for many days. Hope was stronger and they could almost taste the victories of taking back the kingdom. However, for the Princess, her eyes seemed tired and her smiles to the men seemed less true. The decisions she would make once we hit the south seemed to weigh her down and although Olympia chatted into her ear for most of the day, a real smile was a rarity.

Life as a Queen would not be easy.

Sir Coulee fell in step next to me. "Has Princess Seattel talked to you recently?"

My feet hurt and the tiring day had me quite impatient. "I am her personal guard," I reminded the knight. "She talks to me often."

"Fair enough," the knight put his hands up. "I am only wondering as there seems to be something causing her stress." He motioned toward the Princess, marching through the wilderness, followed by an endless stream of words from Olympia. Her hair was braided back, showing the creases on her forehead as she ignored the words of the farm girl next to her, and continued to deeply think about something. "Do you know what is on her mind?"

I knew the Princess too well. She was thinking about the Crown King. My thoughts were confirmed as she threw a quick glance toward the knight in question before continuing her trek. "Perhaps you should ask her," I suggested to the knight.

"I might just do that," Sir Coulee murmured. We continued to walk in silence. The sun was shining brightly through the woods but it was getting late.

A few moments later camp was made in a clearing in the woods. The trip through the desert was rough and many of the men were coughing from dry throats. A group of men headed to the river to fill up the water canteens. I followed the Princess as she headed off with the group, my hand on the hilt of my sword.

The river was close by, only a few hundred steps away. The water was rushing and a small waterfall was in view. Rocks lined the waterfront and the trees shaded half of the flowing river. A few of the men stripped their shirts and waded into the cold, refreshing water. The sun was hot enough that day to give a few of them sunburn. I waited for the Princess to fill her canteen before I followed suit.

She took a gulp of the liquid and sat back. I took a deep breath, filling my lungs with the familiar forest air. Some birds chirped nearby and the laughter of the men echoed around the area as one dunked another beneath the cool water.

"Almost there." She spoke the words softly. I nodded my head, taking another sip of my own water. The Princess dipped her feet into the water. I let my muscles relax as I followed suit, wiggling my toes in the river.

The peaceful moment was short lived.

With a hideous scream, a group of men leapt from the rocks beside the waterfall, making their way quickly down the rivers edge toward our group. I barely had time to stand and yank my sword out before the first bandit struck at me. Yells of warning went out from the other soldiers as they clambered to get out of the water and arm themselves. More men appeared from beside the waterfall, yelling their battle cries as they rushed us.

There were about two men for each of us. Without help from some of the men in the camp, we were doomed.

Chapter 23

I stumbled back from the bashing blow of the crude club which had caught me off guard. Despite my tunic absorbing most of the force of the impact, it sent a wave of blunted pain through my torso.

In a split second, as the scene around me devolved into chaos, shirtless Evergreen soldiers and leather-clad bandits engaging in the melee with complete abandon, I sized my opponent.

His face was smeared with mud and soot, bits of grime and gravel knotted in his matted black hair. His face distorted into a vicious snarl as he gripped his club firmly in his right hand, a dirty cord knotted around his wrist. I thanked myself in that moment that I had not removed my upper garments as so many of my comrades had, as I knew my gambeson to be superior to this bandit's crude vest made of sewed chunks of leather animal hides. I shoved the Princess behind me.

With a shout, I gripped my sword by the hilt with both hands, executing a flourished thrust toward my foe. Perhaps he would be intimidated by flair and prowess.

I was wrong.

The muscular left fist of the bandit slammed into my unprotected cheekbone, and I felt the crackling of his knuckles as my head reeled to the left from his blow. The bandit followed his punch with a swift thrust of his own club, aimed at my left knee, throwing me off balance. As I staggered back, he swung again, but I was ready. My sword met his club with the chopping sound of metal against wood, and I swirled the club free from his hand and onto the ground. My sword-point was facing his exposed gut after that maneuver, and I threw my body's weight behind my sword and I plowed into him. I felt his warm blood and flesh against my hands and the hilt of my sword as the bandit gasped against my ear. Lurching back, I pulled my reddened blade from his abdomen, allowing him to slump to his knees before slamming my knee into his jaw, sending him backwards into the gravel riverside with a sickening thud. He didn't move.

Looking around at the chaos, my eyes caught the Princess cowering by the river, trembling in fear as a bandit rushed past her to slam his weight into an injured Evergreen soldier, sending him sprawling into the shallow riverbank. Her eyes were wide in fear and her hands grasped a rock to use in self defense.

Every nerve tingled. I must guard the Princess.

I rushed to her side, pushing her behind me once again. She clung to my arm and I forced myself to ignore her nails digging into my arm.

This second bandit stomped on the neck of the soldier, snapping it in a swift movement. He whipped his head around, his long blond hair soaked with river water, and roared in fury at the sight of me. I held my sword at the ready, and the brute swung his own sword wildly in my direction. I parried swiftly, hearing the clang of iron and seeing the small splash of rust that arose from his own crude blade as it made contact with mine.

The warmth of the Princess' hand had disappeared.

The weight of his swing caught me off balance, and the bandit lunged forward, knocking me off my feet and onto my back in the water of the riverbank. My sword tumbled from my grasp.

As I swung my hand wildly, searching for the blade, the boot of the bandit slammed into my chest, pushing me into the mud of the riverbank, the cold water wrapping itself about my arms and legs. He lunged forward with his sword, but I rolled aside, grabbing his foot with both hands as I did so, twisting his leg so that he fell into the rocks beside me.

Making it an even playing field, I grabbed a hand-sized rock and bashed it into his face, seeing his cheekbone deform and crack after the second bash. His thick hands grabbed my arm before the third swing, twisting it outwards and away from my body, in an effort to get me to release the rock. My left hand swung deftly to my boot, unsheathing the small dagger I had therein, and plunging it without hesitation into the bandit's thigh. With a roar, he let go of my hand, which was his undoing.

I immediately slammed the rock several times into his exposed neck, feeling and hearing the crunching of his trachea. The bandit gargled and gasped for breath as blood poured out of his open neck and mouth, at which point I pulled myself to my feet and left him to his fate.

Still tense, I pulled Princess Seattel closer to me and farther down the river, eyes scanning the ridge for potential archers. She stumbled in the knee high water.

"You!" a third bandit shrieked, pointing in my direction. "You fight like a Gem! Let me kill you!"

I sized up this third opponent, so focused on my own plight that I was oblivious to the grander strategy of the melee around me. Were we winning or losing? I didn't know. I needed to keep the Princess safe. I glared at the bandit in front of me.

This bandit was different. A smaller figure, about two-thirds my height, a slender frame... and a face more feminine than any highwayman I'd ever seen. She ripped off the bandana and exposed her face. Her raised cheekbones and icy eyes were something to behold.

Around her neck was an elegant necklace of animal teeth, and her fur outfit, while stained with blood and gore, was

more delicate-looking than those of her compatriots. Her sneer
jerked me back to reality though, as she pointed at me again
with her weapon, a strange contraption made of sticks and
chains that hung loosely from her hand. Something I'd never
seen before. All I had in my hand was my dagger. "I want to kill
you, Gem-blade! Don't hold back!"

I heard the gasp of the Princess behind me and every bone in
my body hardened, ready for this next fight. Tightening my grip
on my dagger, I once again made sure the Princess was tucked
behind me before pointing it toward the deranged Gem.

She rushed toward me, swinging her chained contraption in
a wild set of semi-arcs behind her back. I swung my knife, but
she slid below my swing, her feet slamming into my shins, and
her chained contraption wrapping itself around my right hand
with such pressure that I dropped the dagger while my hand
convulsed in pain. She wrenched downward on the chain, and
I fell flat on the ground as she quickly straddled my torso and
slammed her free hand into my face, sending a cyclone of pain
through my jaw and neck.

With my right hand compromised, I swung about wildly with
my left hand, taking hold of the bandit's long auburn hair.
With a wrenching pull on her long hair, I slammed her nose
bridge against my forehead, feeling her nose crack and splinter
against my skull. Her neck within reach, I grappled with my
left hand to take hold of her slender throat, digging in with
my nails as I felt the warm blood seep past my nails and onto

my fingers. With a scream she lunged backwards, letting go of her chained contraption with her other hand, which was still wrapped around my right arm.

My right hand was still so compressed it could hardly move. Instead, I swung my chained right arm like a makeshift club into the waist of the woman, sending her staggering off of me, giving me the moment I needed to lurch to my feet. I wasted no time in swinging my clubbed arm like a chained pendulum into the side of her head, throwing her further off balance as my left hand sent a low punch into her gut.

But as she staggered back, away from me, something in me kept from rushing forward to end her. Her eyes locked with mine, with a fierce enmity I had only ever seen in a mortal combatant intent on ending my life. But at that point, a rousing shout and the thundering of footsteps echoed in my ears, and guards and bandits with one accord looked toward the direction of the sound.

An innumerable swarm of Evergreen soldiers charged the scene, weapons swinging wildly. The bandits began to scatter. In this small distraction, the woman made her move and tried to kick.

"Sir Washeen!"

A rock came flying from the side and crashed into the side of her head. I looked where the throw had come from and saw the Princess pick up another heavy stone from the water. She glared at the Gem warrior, raising her arm to throw the next rock.

She missed.

The Gem spoke, blood dripping from her mouth, "You won't escape Gem-Blade!" Her eyes narrowed and she growled. "You will die by my hand!" Another bandit ran toward the Princess and I, snarling.

The female Gem lunged.

I should have been more prepared. I did not expect her hands to wrap around my throat and her weight to land on me. I sank like a rock to the river floor and struggled against the might of this Gem woman. From having little time to prepare with such an attack, the little air I had left in my lungs ran out and water began seeping in.

The river water rushed past my ear. Was that screaming? My spine molded to the sharp stones underneath. I struggled to get to my knees but the woman had pressure on my limbs, making them impossible to move.

Desperation sunk in and I began panicking. I could care less about my own needs. I was the only one standing between the Princess, this Gem woman, and the bandit.

Suddenly the body pressing on mine disappeared and a hand yanked my arm up. The air was warm compared to the water and I practically swallowed it in desperation. The body of the Gem woman floated past leaving a line of red blood in the water. I shook the hair out of my eyes to see who had defeated the warrior.

Sir Coulee was standing guard in front of the Princess, sword at the ready and eyes narrowing as he watched what Gem warriors were left running for their lives. He skillfully dodged a desperate slice from a passing bandit and with an easy twist of his wrist, ended the man's life with his sword through his gut. The original charging bandit was dead on a rock a few feet away.

I dare not think what would have happened if Sir Coulee had not been there.

I collapsed to my knees to catch my breath, every inhale burning.

The Evergreen Kingdom had won the fight. The Gems and bandits dispersed as quickly as they came and the reinforcing Evergreen soldiers scattered to pursue them.

I looked at the Princess. She was thankfully unscathed; bandits rarely kill potential ransoms. Her hair was matted with mud and river water, and her eyes met mine. The crystal blue look seemed to freeze all the warmth left in me.

"Are you alright, your highness?" I choked out amidst my wheezing.

Her voice was cold. "I am fine, Sir Washeen."

The answer was blunt. I bowed my head slowly toward her and blinked more water out of my eyes. She held her chin high and glanced every now and then toward the knight on her left. He was rinsing the blood off his blade.

"Your majesty," Sir Coulee offered her his arm and she took it gracefully. He led her from the river and to the bank.

I continued to kneel in the water, feeling embarrassment wash over me. The cold of the water no longer bit and I wished my breath would have left my body.

I had failed.

"Your grace!" A yell came from the woods and out stumbled Sir Marhys, sword raised. The knight seemed ready for the fight of his life. "Are you hurt?" Behind him Sir Sumner stabbed a final blow in a bandit.

"I am fine," the soon to be Queen replied. "Thanks to Sir Coulee." Her eyes darted my way for a quick moment before focusing on the conversation before her once again. She knew I had made a foolish mistake and she would have likely paid the ultimate price for my actions if not for Sir Coulee.

The knight nodded back at her. "It was nothing, your majesty. Just doing my duty."

Princess Seattel nodded at the man. Her hair dripped and her wet clothes stuck to her body, leaving not much to be imagined. The knights respectfully only looked at her eyes. Except Sir Coulee.

He glanced downwards.

Although I was ashamed of my error, I could barely contain the anger I felt.

Not one glance was spared in my direction as the knights and the Princess left the area. Some Evergreen soldiers rummaged through the bodies of the Gem warriors in search of gold or weapons, while others dragged the remains into piles to burn. The world seemed to move around me as my entire being remained numb from failure. Water brushed along my skin, erasing any signs of blood and dirt. Darkness began to fall.

"Sir Washeen!"

For a moment I believed I had imagined a voice calling my name. I glanced up and my eyes came to rest on the farmer girl from Thornwood. She stood at the shore.

"Get out of the water!" she yelled at me. "You are going to freeze!"

With a heave I got to my feet. I began making my water towards the bank. My foot hit an item in the water. A glance down showed my metal sword, looking polished and clean from the river water. I had personally received the sword from King Yakima.

Do I leave it in the water?

My fingers were so cold I could hardly wrap them around the familiar hilt of the sword, yet I managed to sheath it before heading toward the bank. Olympia was waiting with a piece of fabric and wrapped it around me as I exited the water.

"Are you alright?" the girl asked. "That must have been a bad battle! Princess Seattel seemed pretty shaken up." She began to lead me back toward camp. "Sir Coulee is also upset." Her eyes scanned mine. "You aren't hurt, are you?"

I shook my head.

"Why were you in the river?" she asked. "Were you not guarding the Princess? Surely you would have accompanied her back to camp."

"I do not think the Princess requires my service any longer," I informed Olympia. Before I could continue speaking, the girl snorted. I raised an eyebrow.

"Of course she does! Just because she has the rest of the army and Sir Coulee next to her now does not mean she has no need for you!"

"He can protect her better than I."

"Maybe," Olympia agreed. She had seen what a skilled knight Sir Coulee was. "But does he know her as well as you? Can he guess how she is going to act amidst the danger? Does he know when she needs to be removed from a scenario or when she needs to sleep? Can he tell when she will lose her temper or when she needs to be sat down to eat?"

I glanced at the girl, wondering what she was getting at.

"I am just saying that perhaps being the guard of the Evergreen Princess does not only mean watching out for her physically in battle," Olympia said. "That is the main part, but you do more than that. You watch her constantly and can predict situations and her needs. You are her friend." She kicked a rock as we walked. "Sir Coulee does not do that."

"She intends to marry Sir Coulee and make him Crown King," I blurted out before I could stop myself. The birds seemed to stop chirping and the breeze held its breath.

Olympia froze mid step. "Really?"

I refused to speak more, already ashamed I had told her something the Princess told me in confidence. Embarrassment swept over me once again as the memories of my other recent failure came back to haunt me. It didn't seem to matter, however, as Olympia continued her talking.

"I do not believe she would," the girl said.

"What do you mean?" I asked.

Her eyes met mine. "There are better men than him."

Chapter 24

"**M**oxee!" The shout echoed through-out the camp. Many of the soldiers smiled as the familiar voice continued to speak. "Come help cook dinner!" Olympia stood next to a big pot and stirred in some veggies as she yelled for the man once again. "Mox-ee!"

"Hurry up Moxee!" one of the soldiers joked. "Do not want to disappoint the missus!" A cackle rose up from the surrounding men.

Olympia huffed. "You all know I have a beloved."

"Sure! Whatever you say!" Moxee chuckled, walking over to the blond haired girl. "I'm beginning to think this 'Kenne' guy is just a story."

"Washeen!" Olympia huffed again. "Tell them!" I glanced up from my post outside the Princess' tent and gave a nod toward the men who were looking at me, confirming that Olympia was indeed telling the truth.

Well, part of it, that is.

Sir Coulee met my eyes as he passed me, exiting the tent. His body language showed that he had heard the conversation from the men.

"Mix this," Olympia instructed Moxee as she stepped away from the fire. "Coulee!" The man flinched at the informal title but turned nonetheless. "How far are we from the rest of the Evergreen army?"

There was a pause as all the men stopped what they were doing and looked at the knight in question. In the last few days, Sir Coulee had grown to be an important voice among the men. A few had seen him defeat the bandits in the river three days back and stories of his fighting skills were whispered as we walked.

Sir Coulee cleared his throat. "We should be there by tomorrow evening." A cheer went up from among the men. Some went back to whittling, some to stories, and the few to their cooking chores given to them by Olympia.

I stood up straight as the tent flap opened again. The rest of the knights, Sir Sumner, Sir Harring, Sir Marhys, and Sir Quincy exited. The Princess peaked her head out. "Sir Washeen." I respectfully bowed my head and entered the tent. In the past, I would have been in the tent alongside the knights, by the Princess' side. However, I felt it was not necessary now that she had four knights next to her.

Sir Coulee included.

I entered the tent and stood at the door with my hand on the hilt of my sword. A familiar stance.

Princess Seattel stood by the table with the map laid out on it. "Do you have anything to say?"

This confused me. "Your majesty?"

She sighed and folded her arms, leaning against the table behind her. Her chopped hair was loose and some of the men found smaller trousers and a tunic to give her. There was almost no comparison between her now and what she was like living in the castle. This Princess was ready for a revenge battle to take back her kingdom. She no longer had studies in the library or tea with the surrounding kingdoms' noblewomen.

"You have not spoken a word to me for three days, Sir Washeen." Her crystal eyes pierced mine and her lips were pulled in a tight line.

I forced myself to meet her eyes. "Yes, your majesty." There was a moment of silence as I did not know what to say next. The Princess sighed and ran a hand through her hair.

"This is about the fight by the river, is it not?"

"Yes, your majesty."

There was another moment of silence and I looked down at the ground. I could hear the Princess shuffling some papers, probably the map on the table, before sighing. "Nobody is perfect. You defended me honorably. You defeated two men." She shuddered with the memories.

"This is true. But you could have died," I practically spat out, angered at myself for what could have been. I gripped the hilt of my sword tighter.

"I would have died long ago had you not been my personal guard," the Princess argued back. "Accept the loss and pride yourself with the wins." We stood and looked at each other. Her words were spoken with honesty and I felt myself relax. I had defeated two of the strongest men of the battle. The Gems who went after the Princess were never easy warriors to defeat.

Princess Seattel sighed. "It is not the same without you always by my side." She shifted her weight and glanced up at me. "I miss it."

Startled, I answered. "Your majesty?"

She took a step closer. "You are more than my personal guard, Washeen." Her voice was soft. She took a step closer. "You, Helen, and I always had a special bond." I watched her carefully as she anxiously folded her hands in front of her. "You are the closest person to me." Sir Coulee crossed my mind and I opened my mouth.

Some of the men outside the tent laughed loudly, stopping our conversation. Olympia's demanding voice argued with one of them. It was something about the stew. I glanced away from Princess Seattel's piercing stare as a shadow moved outside the fabric wall.

A voice was cleared outside the front of the tent and then it spoke. "May I come in, your majesty?" It was Sir Coulee.

"Enter."

The man appeared back into the tent with two bowls of steaming hot stew. It was the only thing we had eaten for days as it was simple enough to cook for such a large group of men. He handed one to the Princess. He did not look at me. "I was wondering if you would like my acquaintance for supper," Sir Coulee asked the soon to be Queen. She smiled brightly at him.

"I would."

I took this as my cue to leave, trying to ignore the fact that the man had interrupted our conversation. I slipped out, undetected I suspect, as Sir Coulee had her attention and was making her giggle. Exiting the tent, Olympia bumped into me. "Oh! Sorry Washeen!"

I nodded at the girl. "It is fine."

She handed me a bowl of stew, leaving one more left in her hands. She motioned toward the bowl. "I thought I would bring some to Seattel." The informalities the girl spoke with often startled the knights and the soldiers, but this time none of them seemed to blink an eye. After traveling a few days with her, I suspected that they were getting used to her ways. Sir Harring still corrected her every now and then.

"She received a bowl from Sir Coulee," I informed the girl. Her face fell, but she quickly masked it with a smile.

"That is okay. I will just give this to Quincy." She nodded her head toward the knight aforementioned. "Do you think Seattel wants to talk to her Advisor tonight?" The girl was proud of the title she had won for herself.

Laughter came from inside the tent. It seemed to answer the question and this time Olympia made no effort to hide the look on her face. Disappointment. Whether it be because Sir Coulee was still in the tent, or because she felt she no longer could talk to Princess Seattel one on one, I do not know. She huffed and walked toward Sir Quincy instead.

I stood my ground by the door of the tent and took a bite of the stew.

I was not needed inside.

The next day's travels went smoothly. Even though Sir Quincy, Sir Sumner, and Sir Marhys arranged the watch schedules, I did not sleep well the night before. Sir Coulee slept as close to the tent as possible, I continued to sleep at the foot of the door. It was apparent the man no longer trusted my guarding abilities as a few times throughout the night he stepped beside what he thought was my sleeping form to take a glance at the Princess and make sure everything was alright.

He did not know that I knew he had done this. One more step into the tent and I would have stopped him. But each time he would return to his sleeping spot and doze off once again.

Laughter jolted me out of my own thoughts. I glared at the scene before me. Sir Coulee had made the Princess laugh once again. Her face no longer held the look of stress and the frown lines had all but disappeared.

Olympia sighed beside me. "I remember when Kenne would make me laugh like that."

This startled me. I did not think Kenne would have had the ability to do so.

Another giggle caused both Olympia and I to look at the Princess once again. This time, Sir Coulee had placed his hand on her upper arm as they walked, telling a wild tale and waving his other arm about. Sir Harring and Sir Sumner were listening to the story closely, but were watching where their feet were taking them instead of where Sir Coulee's hands were.

Not that they would say anything. It was my job to step up if Princess Seattel seemed uncomfortable. But uncomfortable, she was not. She leaned into the touch as they continued to walk.

I could not believe my eyes. One day she hated him and the next he managed to weasel his way into her arms. Each step I took, I stomped the ground harder, as if to somehow catch the attention of the knight before me. My breaths came in short bursts.

She may not remember, but I cannot forget how he lied.

"Surely Kenne must be wondering where I went and when I'll be back," Olympia stated, stepping over a rather large rock that was in the middle of the road. "I hope he is not too worried."

The guilt was so heavy it was hard to breathe. Here I was, blaming Sir Coulee for keeping something from the Princess that was so important, yet I was doing just the same to

Olympia. Surely the King's death is more important than some village leader? Yet, I could not help but cringe at the still lovesick girl next to me.

"He and I used to go for walks in the evening," she rambled on. "He would love to be here and experience this adventure!" She skipped a little, happy with the memories.

I opened my mouth, but then closed it quickly as the thought of betraying another person close to me hurt more than the guilt I felt. Sir Coulee subtly turned his head and looked toward Olympia and I.

He shook his head, then pushed his dark brown hair out of his eyes. My nostrils flared. Apparently the knight was listening in on our conversation. He knew I debated to tell her that her beloved was dead.

I glared back at him and moved my eyes toward his hand which was still present on the Princess' body. He slowly let go and moved it back to his side as they walked. I could see him swallow. Inwardly, I smirked. He must still be respectful toward me as the guard of Princess Seattel.

After all, I had taken down two vicious men before he arrived.

A snap of a branch echoed loudly among the clomping of the men who followed behind the knights. In a moment I had jumped in front of the Princess, sword withdrawn and pointed toward the woods. Sir Coulee followed suit. Princess Seattel placed her hand on my arm and the warmth soaked through my tunic. My eyes scanned for the potential enemy to emerge. My heart was pounding.

The rest of the men quieted.

A rabbit hopped out and scattered across the path. Sir Coulee chuckled and patted my arm. "Glad you still have those reflexes," he smirked at me. The Princess patted my arm and continued to walk forward, Sir Harring offering her conversation. The rest of the men also continued to journey, Olympia falling in step to talk with Moxee.

An overreaction was better than no reaction at all, but yet I felt the heat rush to my face. I forced myself not to show any negative feelings as I sheathed my sword. That was, until Sir Coulee made another comment. "A good knight learns from his mistakes." He began to walk after the Princess. I knew he was also implying about the battle by the river.

"I am not a knight," I snarled at the man.

"I know."

"I am her personal guard."

He stopped in his step. He did not look at me. "You will not be her personal guard forever."

I forced my anger down but still spat out bitterly, "and why not?"

He turned towards me calmly. "Because eventually she will not need you," he stated as if it was the obvious.

I inwardly laughed at the man, knowing he knew not what he was talking about. "She will always need me."

Sir Coulee scoffed, his unknightly behavior once again coming to light. "Did King Yakima have a personal guard?" I knew the answer. "Has Princess Seattel needed you to guard her these last few days?" I knew the answer to that as well. "When she is Queen, she will always have enough knights and guards around her that a personal guard will no longer be necessary." The words cut deep, especially after the conversation I had with the Queen-to-be the day before.

"She may not realize it yet," Sir Coulee continued, ignoring my silence, "but when she does, you will make a fine knight." Even the thought of not being there to protect the Princess almost sent me into a panic. It was a nightmare thinking I would have to rely on others to keep her safe. Did Sir Coulee know something I did not?

"She will not dismiss me, Coulee," I spoke through clenched teeth, firm in my answer though doubts plagued my mind. Sir Coulee just shrugged, sheathed his sword, and walked forward, leaving me to my thoughts. I watched him jog toward the front of the group.

I began to follow. The Princess will always need her personal guard, no matter what Sir Coulee says.

Chapter 25

"I see it!" Olympia's shout of delight overpowered that of the men talking. Everyone rushed to the ridge to look, spotting the smoke and some town houses roofs in the distance. Sunnyside was one of the biggest cities in the Evergreen Kingdom, having a castle as big as the one in Everson. "What a grand view!" Tents around the city had popped up, most likely supporting the troops that had gathered down south as well as any fighting survivors of the Everson Castle attack.

Myself never being to this place before, and Princess Seattel who had only been here as a very small child, gazed out across the area. The Princess breathed deeply, as if taking in the scene and the freshness of Gem-free territory. Storm clouds loomed overhead and I could tell they were ready to burst. I hope we did not have to walk in the rain.

"Let us continue walking!" Sir Harring directed the group loudly, motioning towards the city. We should get there within the hour!" A cheer erupted from the men and getting a second wind in their step, marched down the ridge and toward the city. The wind seemed to push us forward.

Sir Harring was right and within the hour we marched through the city gates and towards the castle. Villagers exited their homes and shops and watched as we walked, smiles on their faces. Night was beginning to fall and a few men stumbled on the loose bricks. Princess Seattel also lost her footing.

I reached out and steadied her, holding onto her arm gently.

Sir Coulee had grabbed her other arm. I kept my face neutral and nodded thanks towards the man, inwardly glaring at his quick reaction.

"Thank you." Perhaps Princess Seattel was talking to both of us and not just Sir Coulee. Yet, she smiled at him.

I turned around from the sounds of happy chatter and saw Olympia practically skipping down the path. She had declared before how excited she was to be going to a castle, something she only would dream of back in her farming village.

The castle was enormous, although not as grand as the one back in Everson. There were vines tangling their way up the castle bricks and painted glass windows with beautiful images in the walls. The lanterns had been lit and cast shadows along the castle walls, causing them to look even bigger than what they were.

"Your majesty!" A knight rushed forward out of the castle and bowed before the Princess. His green cape fluttered perfectly behind him, showing his long life as a knight. "We are so grateful that you are alive and well!" His gray hair was noticeable, even with the fading light. "I am Sir Spoka, the head knight here at Sunnyside Castle. I last saw you when you were a child." A few more knights had come through the castle doors as well and were now bowing in front of the soon to be Queen.

"Rise," Princess Seattel instructed. The men rose from the cobblestones and awaited further instruction. "We have a lot to discuss," the Princess informed the knight. "But first, let us get these soldiers situated." She motioned behind her toward the group of men.

"Indeed," he agreed. "I have assembled the troops outside the city and set up a few tents for any more fighting men that have retreated from the Everson Castle." As the man began to explain a huge list of tasks and assignments that needed to be done the next day, Olympia poked my arm.

I ignored it.

She poked it again. "Washeen!" she whispered. I sighed and turned to look at the girl, knowing if I ignored her again she would just continue poking me. She motioned toward the Princess. "Would it not be better for her to rest so she has a fresh mind to start tomorrow?"

I looked back at Princess Seattel and noticed that although she was holding her head up high and walking how royalty would, there was a slight weariness to the way she was moving and the smile she gave the head knight. My own feet and legs were hurting and I was used to standing all day.

"As her personal guard," I mumbled back to Olympia, "I simply watch out for any physical signs of danger." I paused and I could see the blond haired girl try to piece together what I was saying. "If her Advisor told her to rest..." I never finished my sentence, for Olympia gasped.

"I can not talk to her in front of all these knights!" she whispered toward me.

I was careful to not take my eyes off the Princess, neither agreeing or disagreeing with her statement. "You are her Advisor."

Olympia gulped. Then, after a few hesitant steps, she approached the Princess, who was deep in conversation with Sir Spoka. Sir Harring and Sir Marhys also approached from organizing the soldiers. They had all turned and headed toward the tents that were pitched outside the city.

"Are you mad?" Sir Coulee hissed from my left. "This is no time for her to play Advisor."

The knight watched nervously as the farmer girl placed her hand on the Princess' shoulder. Instantly, the conversation ceased. The knights from Sunnyside Castle gasped. Sir Spoka was startled, looking between the Princess and the blond haired girl.

"Seattel, do you not think we should sleep for the night and start fresh tomorrow?" Olympia spoke to the soon to be Queen. Another gasp went up from the knights and a few started murmuring among themselves. "You must be exhausted. This can be spoken about tomorrow." Sir Spoka began babbling in shock.

"This is not good," Sir Coulee shook his head. "She should know formalities by now." I know it had always irked the man when Olympia simply called him 'Coulee', but in the farmer girl's defense, that was the way she was brought up and raised. There were no titles in either of her villages.

Princess Seattel acted exactly as I had predicted. She simply nodded towards the girl, grateful for the reminder of her aching feet, then turned toward Sir Spoka. "My Advisor is right. We should sleep for the night and return to these discussions early tomorrow." Olympia stifled a yawn behind her. A cold breeze swept through the courtyard, causing the Princess' hair to fly back, the chopped sections looking ragged.

Although Sir Coulee did not say anything, I could tell by his rigid body behavior he was not happy the Princess entertained her Advisor by answering her.

Not knowing how to act with such a display, Sir Spoka bowed his head. "As you wish, my Princess," he stammered. "I will show you personally to your room." He looked around at Sir Harring, Sir Marhys, Sir Sumner, Sir Quincy, Sir Zillah, and Sir Coulee. "If you all follow Sir Cordos, he will take you to your rooms."

Sir Coulee hesitantly followed his fellow knights, darting a look at Princess Seattel. Whether she saw it or not, she did not act on it. Instead, her eyes met mine and I nodded at her.

I would not leave her side.

"I can have another room prepared for your Advisor," the knight stuttered once again, taking in the dirtiness of the farmer girl's clothes. "I did not realize you had already appointed one." Olympia smiled nervously at the man, clearly not comfortable with the looks he had given her as well as sleeping alone in a room in an unknown castle.

"She will be fine in my room," Princess Seattel informed the man. He bowed once again and led us to the sleeping quarters.

After a quick bath, new clothes, and a hearty dinner of pork, berries, and bread, the Princess yawned and climbed into a bed that was loaded with blankets and pillows. I had taken my own quick bath and received a new change of clothes myself. The warm crackling fire was the perfect lullaby and soon both she and Olympia had drifted off into a blissful sleep.

I stood from my seated position by the fire and placed another log in before snuffing out the candles on the table. I opened the door, ready to find sleeping quarters myself. Instead, a voice called out to me. "Washeen." It was the Princess.

"Your highness?"

"Stay."

The lanterns flickered in the hallway and cold air blew in past the door. The fireplace in the Princess' room was so warm and inviting and I hated to leave such a comfortable position. I knew she was safe in this room as I had personally handpicked soldiers from our group to stand watch throughout the night.

There was no reason for me to stay.

"Please." It was not an order she was giving. She was asking.

"My Princess." I moved closer to the bed where she held out a pillow and a blanket. No other words were needed as I took the items and laid them on the rug in front of the fireplace.

Quietly, I took off my belt and tunic and draped them over a chair. My boots came off next and I wiggled my toes, stretching them. I placed the blanket down, slid the sword underneath my pillow, and made myself comfortable, turning my head so I could see the Princess from where I was laying.

There were a few moments of silence and I would have believed the Princess was back asleep if not for the flames illuminating her open eyes.

"Washeen?"

"Yes, my Princess?"

She paused for a moment, turning her eyes toward the girl laying next to her. Confirming that she was sleeping, Princess Seattel continued to speak.

"Tomorrow will be a busy day," she sighed, speaking in low tones to not wake Olympia. "There are many things to discuss." She waited, as if to allow me to speak, but I held my tongue. "War plans, the Crowning Ceremony," she hesitated a moment, "and of course a wedding during the ceremony when I decide on a Crown King."

The wood crackled in the fireplace and shadows danced around the room. I spoke. "Have you decided?"

There was some shuffling of her blankets. I was not ready for her answer. "Yes."

My blood went cold although the heat of the fire warmed my body. "Sir Quincy?" I asked hopefully, holding my breath, but knowing that she had barely spoken to the knight in the last few days. He would make an excellent king.

"No."

My heart lurched and I swallowed. "Do you remember the last conversation you had with your father, Princess?" I questioned. There was silence. "He stated, 'Love comes second. The kingdom comes first.'" I pulled the blankets up closer to my neck.

"I know," came the whisper.

"Are you going to marry this nobleman for love? Or for the Evergreen Kingdom?" I knew that personally, Princess Seattel was against marriage if it was not someone who she loved. That was the reason why her and her father had spoken harsh words the night of the attack.

Her voice was quiet, yet she answered with a bold sound as if to convince herself, as well as me. "I believe the love will come in time." My heart was beating hard and loud. I took a few deep breaths in an effort to slow it lest the Princess would hear.

"And if it does not?"

My question seemed to float in the air. No answer was given for quite a while, although her crystal eyes did not stray from mine. There were some footsteps moving in the hallway as the guards changed. The stained glass window creaked from the blowing wind outside. Rain began to patter.

"Then my father was right," she all but whispered. "I must marry for the Evergreen Kingdom first." Lightning flashed outside as the storm finally broke. The window rattled as the thunder let out a deafening roar. "My father did approve of him after all."

I spoke the question I already knew, but was dreading the answer too. "Who will you ask to become Crown King?"

I did not get nightmares often, but the name she spoke filled my bones with dread. I felt cold inside. The flames of the fire crackled loudly and echoed around the room.

"Sir Coulee."

I showed no emotion. I did not dare to move. I hardly breathed. Sir Coulee.

Her eyes were still on me, seemingly piercing my skull and reading my thoughts. Yet, all she said was, "Goodnight, Washeen."

I swallowed. "Goodnight, my Princess."

Epilogue

The next few days were chaotic. The army had to be prepared, there were meetings with representatives from Beaverland as they had sent troops to help take the Evergreen Kingdom back, and there was a great fuss about the Crowning Ceremony, as well as the wedding portion.

I walked through the familiar castle hallways on the third day since we arrived, escorting Princess Seattel to another council meeting. The servants, maids, knights, and noblemen bowing as we walked by almost seemed familiar once again. All the scratches and bruises from the long journey had disappeared from her skin and the day before she finally had time to sit down and have her hair trimmed proper. The wavy black locks now rest on the back of her neck, pinned back by a few brooches. For the first time in a long while, she was dressed in a silky green gown, its hem dusting the floor.

She looked like the Princess of the Evergreen Kingdom, once again.

"Thank you." She turned to me. "It will be a longer moment or so. Go find yourself something to eat." I nodded, my stomach growling. Yet, I made sure she was seated at the table before leaving the council room.

Green capes fluttered past me, as well as yellow, with both Evergreen knights and Beaverland knights preparing for the journey north to fight. Servants walked by with flowers and maids scrubbed the floors until they shone. There were many lanterns glittering in the hallways and elegant forest green curtains being hung around the castle walls. The castle seemed to hum with excitement.

I rounded the corner to the Princess' room and stopped in my tracks. Sir Coulee stood by the door with flowers and was knocking politely. I backed up into a small corridor and watched as the door was opened.

Olympia looked down at the flowers then back up at Sir Coulee. "Yes?"

Sir Coulee looked rather disappointed to see the farmer girl answer the door of his future Queen's room, but spoke nonetheless. "Is Princess Seattel here?"

Olympia beamed brightly, yet her smile didn't quite reach her eyes. "No, she had to step out for a council meeting." There had been more than a few in the last three days, with the council mainly consisting of the knights who had traveled with her and a few rich noblemen of the area. I did not know the latter ones. Even mealtimes were busy with talks of plans and actions. Princess Seattel had no time to herself and the few moments she did, Sir Coulee was there.

Sir Coulee looked taken back. I suspected he was confused as to why he was not called to this particular meeting. As the future Crown King, he usually attended all such affairs next to the Queen to be herself. He shook off the thought and spoke again. "I will come back at a later time."

I quickly threw myself back against the wall as the knight turned to walk away. "Coulee! I mean, uh, Sir Coulee!" Olympia called after him. I peaked back around the corner and the knight turned back to her.

"Yes?"

Olympia wrung her hands nervously in front of the man, an action I had never seen her do before. "I hate to be a bother," she started, "but I was wondering if you could arrange some sort of escort for me to go back to Thornwood after the Crowning Ceremony." She did a small smile toward the knight. "Seattel is so busy right now and I would hate to add another thing to her mind. And as the future Crown King I thought it would be best to request this of you." A few servants walked past me, glancing in my direction with confusion, but ultimately 'ignored' my presence.

I was not acting very honorable.

"Princess Seattel," the man corrected her patiently. "And about the escort," Sir Coulee shifted uncomfortably. "I have been meaning to discuss that with you." My entire being when cold.

"I only need one or two soldiers to help me find my way," Olympia quickly supplied, guessing that the man was going to say that all the men were needed to take back the Evergreen Kingdom. "Not even a horse. I walked here and I can walk back."

"It is not that," Sir Coulee informed the girl. He quickly surveyed the hallway. "Perhaps we should talk inside?" He motioned toward the room and Olympia nodded. A few maids were cleaning the stained glass windows on the far side of the hallway and were whispering. Whether it was about the conversation the knight was having with the farmer girl, or the flowers that it looked like he brought her, I do not know.

They moved inside the room, yet left the wooden door open a crack. I suspected this was intentional, so no rumors would spread. All I knew was that I had to hear this conversation.

The maids picked up their water bucket and walked toward the next window and out of sight. The hallway was clear. I held the hilt of my sword so that it would not make noise as I crept towards the door, careful to land my feet on the floor softly.

"Kenne probably is missing me!" I heard Olympia tell Sir Coulee. "And I am ready to go home now. The garden is most likely overgrown and I am sure all his clothes need washing!" She let out a giggle at the memory of her beloved. "He never was very good at scrubbing them clean."

I crouched carefully, holding back my tunic from showing in the opening of the door, where both the knight and farmer girl could catch a glimpse of it. Instead, I peered around the door and watched the conversation in the reflection of the window.

"Kenne is not waiting for you to come back," Sir Coulee mumbled, picking some of the flowers apart in the bouquet. "He is not missing you." My chest clenched at those words, memory flashing back to Sir Coulee coming out of Thornwood without the village leader at his side.

"What do you mean?"

Sir Coulee refused to look at the girl. "Remember how Sir Washeen and I went to find Kenne at the pub?"

Olympia nodded slowly. "Yes."

"He was selling out the Princess' location to the Gems." I could practically smell the nauseating sweat that the men's body emitted and the liquor that was drunk in the pub.

Olympia laughed suddenly and Sir Coulee's head snapped up to look at the farmer. "Coulee, I never took you as the joking type!" she informed the man. The humor on her face was clear, while Sir Coulee looked ashamed.

He did not correct her on the formalities. Instead, he placed the flowers on the table. "I slayed the Gems, but not before one of the brutes stabbed Kenne."

"So you took him to the village physician?" Olympia filled in the rest. "You are telling me that Belling had to heal him?" She nervously chuckled, not allowing her mind to guess what really happened that night. "He is an excellent physician."

"He did not make it," Sir Coulee blurted out before the farmer girl could continue. I flinched in surprise at the knight, never witnessing him act in such a manner. "I killed the Gem, but by the time I got to Kenne and tried to stop the bleeding, it was no use. He was already gone." The words seemed to tumble out of the man's mouth, the feeling of conviction surpassing the calm manner of which he usually spoke. "I did not mean to keep this from you."

Olympia had gone sheet white. Her hand trembled as she pushed some hair out of her face. "Kenne is waiting for me."

"No." The guilt-ridden man swallowed hard.

"He is. We built a house together." Her voice was small.

"He is not." Sir Coulee cleared his throat and the man awkwardly fumbled with a loose string on the hem of his tunic. "I am sorry." The silence was deafening. I could barely breathe, a combination of the guilt I felt and the fear of the two hearing my breaths.

"You lied to me?"

Sir Coulee was silent. He did not meet her eyes. I shifted my weight.

Olympia's shock turned to anger. "You did not think of telling me this sooner?"

"I did not know how."

"Did not know how, or did not want to?"

There was silence as the man debated his answer, none of them being the right one. The only sound was the flames crackling in the fireplace. Olympia glared at the so-called knight in front of her, rage filling her eyes and her lips pulled tight into a scowl.

"Get out!" Sir Coulee practically darted to the door and I quickly moved back into my original listening spot. Fortunately, the hallway was clear and no ears or eyes would be witness to this encounter.

"Olympia, I-"

"You are a coward!" She spat through clenched teeth. If he were not the future Crown King, I would have placed a gamble that the girl would have slapped the knight's face. Sir Coulee flinched at the harshness, yet took the insult that the girl had spoken without a word. I could tell the knight wanted to say something, yet he kept his mouth closed. "A coward and a liar!"

My guess was he was feeling just as ashamed as I.

There was another long moment of no speaking before Olympia burst into hot tears.

"Princess Seattel will hear about this!" the girl seethed, focused more on the fact that Sir Coulee had lied to her and not that her beloved was dead. "She may think that you are perfect for Crown King but I do not!"

"Watch your tongue!" Sir Coulee snapped at the girl, not wanting the threat on his future to be taken so lightly.

I hope to never see Olympia furious again. Her face was red and her nostrils flared at the knight before her. "The day I will watch my tongue is the day you will stop lying."

The heavy wooden door was slammed in Sir Coulee's face as the Advisor chose her privacy over facing the knight. A muffled sob echoed in the brick hallway. Sir Coulee looked down at his flowers, now wilting after observing the depressing conversation. He dropped them by the door and with what dignity he had left, exited the area.

I pulled away from the wall, forcing myself to wear a stoic face as I walked away from the scene I had just witnessed. My feet seemed to drag, yet I forced myself into my room which was around the corner.

The bread and grapes on the table looked unappetizing.

Ingram Content Group UK Ltd.
Milton Keynes UK
UKHW020729060623
422954UK00015B/888